I was sure the picture had to be the link…but what if I was wrong?

I shuddered and dropped the picture, creating a small crack in the glass, but that wasn't good enough. I picked it up and threw it hard—so hard that the glass shattered. I grabbed the picture frame, shook the broken glass into the trash bin, and then dropped it back on the ground, exposing the picture of my innocent four-year-old face to the steam of lighter fluid that I poured all over it. The light sprinkle continued. *I have to hurry.*

Suddenly, I heard a girlish giggle behind me. My neck tingled, and I jerked my arm, pulling the flame away from the picture. I stood and searched the empty backyard. The sound was so quiet, I almost talked myself into thinking it never happened. But I could feel her. I knew she was here. I spun around and knelt to the ground. With my heart pounding, I quickly touched the flame to the picture and watched the fire spread—racing, glowing, dancing—from the image of my neatly folded hands in my lap to the bow in my light brown hair.

A second later, the fire let out a "wooomp," and I watched the flames settle in to do what I needed them to do—destroy. But while I watched the flames fight the light sprinkling rain, a fear that I kept in the back of my mind started to surface.

Fifteen-year-old Jenna Moores is struggling with her father's recent death. Not long after his passing, a ghost from her childhood returns. When she was young, Jenna's father convinced her that the ghost was just her imagination and that he would always protect her. But now he's gone, the ghost is back, and Jenna knows she's not imagining it. As the entity grows stronger, its threats move from alienating Jenna from her friends and family to killing her. Alone and afraid, she must find and destroy the link that holds the spirit to this world...before Jenna, too, becomes a ghost.

KUDOS for *Ghost in the Blue Dress*

In *Ghost in the Blue Dress* by R. A. Slone, Jenna Moores is a teenager haunted by a ghost. A malicious one. The ghost is the spirit of a young girl who died in the hose where Jenna and her widowed mother live. But when they move to a new house in a new state, the ghost follows. Whenever Jenna tries to get help, the ghost attacks and injures whoever tries to help her. Jenna knows she must destroy the ghost or everyone she cares about is in danger. But how? As YA horror stories go, this is a good one. Slone's character development is excellent and you feel Jenna's pain as she spirals into depression when the ghost gets the upper hand. For YA and new adults who like mild horror, this is a sure-fire hit. ~ *Taylor Jones, Reviewer*

Ghost in the Blue Dress by R A Slone is a coming of age story with a little something more. Our heroine, Jenna Moores, has just lost her father when the book opens. She is also dealing with a child entity she calls the ghost in the blue dress, but unlike a lot of child ghosts, this one is malevolent. Jenna ends up bruised and injured until her doctor thinks that her mother is abusing her. But how does she tell anyone the perpetrator is a ghost, especially when everyone she tells ends up critically injured? Jenna knows that if she doesn't destroy the ghost soon, it will eventually kill her and everyone she cares about. Ghost in the Blue Dress is a well-written tale of courage, determination, and defying the odds. It's as uplifting as it is chilling, a book that will appeal to YA, new adults, and adults alike. ~ *Regan Murphy, Reviewer*

ACKNOWLEDGEMENTS

I owe a huge thank you to my friend Andrea Freeman who pushed me to turn my short story into a novel. Without her enthusiasm and confidence in me, this book would never have been written.

Also, I would like to thank beta readers Beth Munk, Young Adult Author Darcy Vance, Chris Jack, and Author Kathleen Palm.

I would also like to thank my niece Sydney Robbins plus the members of Summit City Scribes of Fort Wayne, Eckhart Public Library Writing Group, and Kendallville Public Library Adult Department Creative Writing Program for their help and feedback.

Thank you to the awesome editors and staff at Black Opal Books.

Also, thanks to Margie Lawson and her writing classes, which boosted my writing from blah to publishable.

GHOST IN THE BLUE DRESS

R. A. Slone

A Black Opal Books Publication

GENRE: YA/NEW ADULT/GHOST/HORROR/PARANORMAL

This is a work of fiction. Names, places, characters and incidents are either the product of the author's imagination or are used fictitiously, and any resemblance to any actual persons, living or dead, businesses, organizations, events or locales is entirely coincidental. All trademarks, service marks, registered trademarks, and registered service marks are the property of their respective owners and are used herein for identification purposes only. The publisher does not have any control over or assume any responsibility for author or third-party websites or their contents.

GHOST IN THE BLUE DRESS
Copyright © 2015 by R. A. Slone
Cover Design by Jackson Cover Designs
All cover art copyright © 2015
All Rights Reserved
Print ISBN: 978-1-626942-97-4

First Publication: JULY 2015

Published by Black Opal Books **http://www.blackopalbooks.com**

DEDICATION

For my husband, Rusty Robbins.
Also for my parents Dewey and Nancy Slone.
Thank you for always believing in me.

CHAPTER 1

Even though the sun was shining bright, darkness covered my heart. Dad's casket lay beneath the small tent, ready to be placed deep in a dark hole once we left Crown Hill Cemetery. Most of my friends and family had made their way to the dinner at the church, but I couldn't leave yet.

Mom walked to the TrailBlazer with Mrs. Vanderley, our family friend and neighbor. I stood with my best friend Tamara behind the row of folding chairs where I'd sat during the graveside sermon.

"I thought he'd always be there for me," I said in a low voice. A strong summer breeze blew a strand of brown hair into my face. I brushed it away.

Tamara gently wrapped her arm in mine. "Let's go, Jenna."

I stared at the casket, my heart numb. Clouds covered the sun. Shadows emerged. Something stirred in the shade of the trees across the cemetery. "Did you see that?" I asked.

Tamara craned her neck. "See what?"

An uneasy feeling had taken root the day Dad died. Something wasn't right. And that something was hiding in the darkness.

ↄ·ↄ·ↄ

A week later, Tamara and I lounged on floating air mattresses in her pool. Her parents were at work. Mom was at home.

I hated to leave her, but I needed to talk to my best friend. Only she'd understand what I was feeling.

"Do you ever get that feeling that someone's watching you?" I asked and looked at her. We lay on our stomachs facing each other.

Her arms were crossed with her chin propped on top. I couldn't tell if she was looking at me for sure because of her reflective sunglasses, but when she tightened her lips, I knew she was thinking. "You mean when someone's staring and you look just in time to catch them?"

I shrugged a shoulder. "Kind of, but more like you look but there's no one there." I hoped that didn't sound too crazy. But Tamara was okay with crazy. That's why I wanted to talk to her about it.

"Um…not really that I know of. Why?"

"Ever since Dad's funeral, I've had some weird feelings, I guess."

"Like what?" she asked. Her eyebrows shot up from beneath her sunglasses, and her voice dropped. "Do you think it could be your dad's ghost?"

I paused. "No. No, it isn't Dad," I said. I hadn't even considered the possibility, because I was talking about something else.

Or should I say *someone* else?

"How do you know?" Tamara asked and carefully rolled onto her back without falling into the pool.

I did the same and sighed. *Do I answer her? Do I tell her that I'm afraid in my own house?* Now that we weren't face-to-face, the urge to tell her had faded. I needed to see her expression when I told her what happened when I was four years old. I needed to know if she believed me.

"Jenna?" Tamara said and kicked chlorinated water at me.

"What?"

"I asked, how do you know?"

"I just do."

જ∾જ

The next morning, I stood in the kitchen waiting for Mom to leave for work. It was her first day back since the funeral. I waited awkwardly, not sure what to say.

"Jenna, honey, could you do some laundry today?" Mom asked and grabbed her car keys and black Rosetti purse from the kitchen counter. She paused for a moment before she leaned in for a hug. I inhaled her perfume, sweet and flowery, the perfume Dad had given her for her birthday before he passed away.

"Okay," I said. I wrapped my arms around her and squeezed. The sweet smell made the pain of losing Dad worse this morning. My throat tightened. Emptiness filled my chest, and I couldn't let her go.

"Love you," she whispered against my hair.

I swallowed a lump. I didn't want her to leave, really. I didn't want to be alone today. Tamara had to go with her older brother, who now had his driver's license, to help their grandma clean her garage. And my other friends were too far away to get there on my own. I wished I were sixteen already. This September couldn't come fast enough.

Mom broke the hug and squeezed my shoulders. "I have to go, honey."

"Okay. Love you," I said. She kissed my cheek, gave me a *we're-going-to-get-through-this* smile, turned, and left.

e/ɔe/ɔ

Later that morning, I decided to brew myself a cup of

coffee. Most of my other fifteen-year-old friends liked tea or lattes, but for me, it was the smell. For as long as I could remember the house always smelled like coffee in the morning. Dad's coffee.

I poured a ton of hazelnut creamer into the cup before I added the coffee and watched the colors swirl together to form a beautiful light brown.

With my cup full, I started up the stairs to my room, taking my time, sipping my coffee. After only a couple of steps, a strange heaviness overtook the air, like the coming of a bad thunderstorm.

I paused, lowered my cup.

A strange glow appeared at the top of the staircase. Small and bright blue. The glowing figure took a moment, but it slowly transformed into something I recognized—recognized and feared.

Pain shot through my chest as if my heart had stopped beating. Weakness spread through my legs and arms and, finally, to my hands. My cup slipped from my grip. Hot coffee spilled all over the carpet and splashed my bare legs.

The form brightened for a moment and then dimmed, pulsating. Eyes shimmered like embers from a fire. We stood for a moment, staring at each other. I felt like I was a child again. The ghost hadn't changed from what I could remember. Blonde, wavy hair, and she wore that same little dress.

My dress.

Her brightness started to fade like a light bulb on a dimmer switch. She flickered on and off. The glow of her eyes faded. And then she vanished.

Numb, I stumbled backward to the bottom of the stairway. My legs, weak and rubbery like I'd ran a marathon, were unable to hold me up any longer. With both hands on the banister, I lowered myself until I sat on the bottom step of the stairway. The same step I sat on when Dad found me crying when I was four years old. The same step where everything had first started.

I wrapped my arms around the banister, and I realized something. I realized Dad was wrong when he told me that I imagined the ghost in the blue dress. That I had imagined her transforming a picture of me into a picture of her, changing my hair, changing my face, unfolding her small hands to crawl out of the frame and into the darkness of the living room. And most of all, that I imagined her evil smile. At the age of four, I believed him. But now he was gone.

And the ghost was back.

e/ɔe/ɔ

I was still sitting on the bottom step of the stairway when the sound of a screen door slamming and a little dog barking caught my attention. I focused on the front door. It was only a few steps away.

Mrs. Vanderley, my neighbor, had just let her black

miniature poodle, Pepe, outside for a morning break. Before I really thought about it, I stood and hurried outside.

I stood on the top step, a little confused. The mid-morning sun was warm. Pepe trotted over to greet me. I wanted to squat and stroked the fur on his back, but I couldn't move yet. He let out a yip and ran back into his yard to do his business.

A large birch tree stood in front of Mrs. Vanderley's house and the sidewalk. Houses lined both sides of the street here in Indianapolis, Indiana. Most of the houses on my block were built in the early 1900s.

The July sun broke through the tree leaves. I stood, waiting for things to make sense again. I wanted to believe that the ghost I saw was my crazy imagination, just like Dad had told me all those years ago. Only the pain in my chest and the residual numbness wouldn't allow me to believe that. What I'd seen was real, and I needed to tell somebody—now.

I reached for my phone to text Tamara about what I'd just seen. Would my other friends laugh at me, though? We'd watched those reality TV ghost-hunting shows before, but I wasn't sure who believed, who didn't, and who would think I was crazy. But my phone wasn't there. My pocket was empty. I guessed I didn't have to make that decision since my phone was in my room charging.

I sighed, not sure what to do. Then I heard Mrs. V calling for Pepe, and I had another idea. Tamara was with her grandma today. Mrs. V had known me for so long and we were so close that she was practically like my own grandma.

I hurried across the yard and to her front step. "Hi, Mrs. V," I said out of breath.

"Well, hello, dear."

"I *really* need to talk with you."

She opened the door for me and Pepe. "Come on in and take a seat. Looks like we need some hot chocolate," she said and left for the kitchen. Whenever I seemed frazzled or upset, hot chocolate was Mrs. V's cure-all.

A few short minutes later, she returned with a cup of steaming goodness. I reached out and took the shiny, ivory cup from her hands.

"Oh, dear. You're shaking," she said and draped a light afghan over my shoulders, even though it was the middle of July. I wasn't cold, but the afghan did feel nice. I sat on an emerald green couch in Mrs. V's living room. She took a seat next to me. I held the cup of hot chocolate she'd made for me with both hands and watched the miniature marshmallows tremble.

Pepe jumped onto Mrs. V's lap and scooted, so his front paws rested on my leg. I thought it was a little weird that Pepe always knew when something was wrong, like he could read minds. I just hoped at this moment he couldn't read mine.

"Now tell me, Jenna," Mrs. V said, her voice soft and slightly shaky from age. "What happened?"

I took in a breath and looked around the living room, not sure what to say. This was Mrs. V, though. I could tell her anything. She had been there for me for so many things, like when Tamara and I fought, which happened more than I liked to admit.

When Mom and I fought, which also happened more than I liked to admit. And, most of all, when Dad died. She was there for me, just like I knew she'd be there for me now.

"Mrs. V?" I asked in a soft voice.

"Yes, dear?"

"I've got a question for you." I fiddled with the handle of my hot chocolate mug.

She made a "hmmm" sound that always meant for me to continue.

"Do you believe in life after death?" I asked and made eye contact.

No flash of doubt crossed her face. I thought she might've had a little bit of a *you're-a-crazy-girl* look, but she didn't. She didn't even hesitate before she asked, "You mean heaven and hell?"

Relieved, I continued. "No—I mean more like ghosts, like not making it to where you're supposed to go."

Pepe shifted to his side, still on her lap, and let out a little sigh. After a moment Mrs. V answered, "You know, I'm not really sure. I guess I don't have a straight answer."

"Well, I can say for sure that I believe in ghosts."

Mrs. V raised her eyebrows. "And why's that?"

"Because I just saw one."

CHAPTER 2

That evening, when Mom got home from work, we sat at the dinner table to eat Chinese takeout. Mom didn't feel like cooking, again. Even if I had known, I wouldn't have spent time in the house alone to fix dinner. Not after what happened this morning. I had stayed the rest of the day at Mrs. V's.

I sat in a different chair, Dad's old chair. That way I faced the living room and the bottom of the staircase. I really couldn't see the bottom step of the stairs because of the kitchen wall, but I felt better knowing that if the ghost appeared, I'd see it instead of letting it sneak up behind me.

Chills popped up on the back of my neck and I fought the urge to spin around and look.

I passed the Emperor's Chicken to Mom. She took

the box and spooned out another helping and set the box on the table.

"Mom?" I asked, my voice soft, unsure. Should I tell her about the ghost? Would she believe me?

"What?" she asked in an *I'm-not-really-here* kind of way.

I paused, waiting for her to look at me, but she didn't. She had that faraway look in her eyes that she would take on for a few days and then shake off. She'd been that way since Dad got sick.

I sighed. She wasn't going to make eye contact with me. Even if I did tell her what happened today, I didn't think she'd really get it. So, I said, "Nothing. Just wondered if I could go to Tamara's tomorrow." Even if my friend thought I was crazy, I was going to tell her about the ghost.

"That's fine, honey. Make sure to be careful. You know that," Mom said. Her gaze never left the wall.

After dinner, I cleared the table and put the dishes in the dishwasher. I didn't want to, but I did anyway.

"Honey?" Mom called from the living room. "My neck is sore. Could you heat up my rice pack?"

I hit a few buttons on the microwave and waited. Once it beeped, I pulled the floral-patterned rice pack from the microwave and carried it through the kitchen. I stopped short of the stairs. I waited for a minute, which made things worse. Now I didn't think I could do it. Maybe I could lean just enough to look—

"Honey?"

My heart jumped into my throat.

"What?"

Mom stared at me from the living room. "What are you doing?"

"Nothing," I said and hurried past the bottom of the stairway. I shot a quick glance to my right.

No ghost.

I handed the warm rice pack to Mom and sat on the couch. *Wheel of Fortune* was on. I sat a little closer to her than normal. I could see the second floor balcony and the top of the stairway to the right, the last place I'd seen the ghost. I swallowed a few times, trying to force my heart back down to where it should be, but it was stuck.

℮⁊℮⁊

The next morning, I poured myself a bowl of Honey Nut Cheerios. I pushed my long, dark brown ponytail off my shoulder and out of my way and sat in Dad's chair to eat. I'd made it to my room last night without anything happening, and I'd made it down the stairs this morning. Maybe yesterday was it. Maybe I'd never see the ghost in the blue dress again.

Still, after breakfast, I was going to text Tamara and spend the day at her house. I rinsed my bowl and put it in the dishwasher, put some Cascade in, and flipped it on. The counters needed cleaned, and I swept the floor, something Mom had asked me to do this morning. *In just a few hours, I'll be soaking up the sun.*

I put the broom back in the corner and started for my room. Anxiety rolled in the pit of my stomach, but I pushed forward. Once I made it up the stairway, the anxious feeling subsided. She wasn't here. Maybe I was right. Maybe yesterday was a fluke, and I'd never see her again.

When I got to my room, I picked up my hot-pink cell phone and texted Tamara. I tossed the phone on the bed and rummaged through the dresser drawer for my turquoise bikini and faded red beach towel. I slipped on a pair of white cotton shorts and flip flops, picked up my phone, and then sat on my bed, waiting for Tamara to respond.

A minute later, a strange noise came from outside my bedroom door, quiet at first. I tilted my head. It almost sounded like a child singing. A slow chill built at the base of my neck.

The singing continued. Every few seconds, something rattled or clinked together, like the child was playing with something. But I wasn't sure. I had to look. I stood and walked to the door, cracking it to peer down the hall to the balcony. Nothing. I opened it a little farther to get a better view of the balcony and stairs. Still nothing.

The singing continued. With the door open, the notes of the song flowed into the room. The chills at the base of my neck trickled down my arms and legs. But I didn't see anything. It had to be the ghost.

The volume increased, as if someone were turning up a radio.

I held my breath, listening. The volume increased again, growing louder and louder and louder. It took me a second to realize it wasn't growing louder.

It was coming closer.

The chills turned into something hot, like lava flowing down my neck and over my body. Was I going to burst into flames? I slammed the door shut and locked it. I locked it against a ghost.

I ran to the window and shoved it open. I looked out. The ground was too far away. My Cheerios pushed up the back of my throat. I swallowed hard and shoved against the screen. It didn't budge.

The eerie singing crept closer to my bedroom door. Heat spread from the base of neck into my arms and down my back. *Think. Think. Think.*

Should I break the screen and jump? I could easily break my leg.

Should I turn around and face the ghost? *I'm too scared.*

What should I do? Frantically, I glanced around my room. Since I couldn't do anything else, I ran to the closet and hid, just like I would if I were four years old again.

                      ʗɔʗɔ

After hiding for what seemed like an eternity, the chills and nausea finally passed. I sat on the floor of my closet and waited for the weird singing sound to start again. But it didn't. The closet door creaked a little when I opened it to look.

I listened. I heard a distant lawn mower, cars on the street, a screen door slamming, and a voice—Mrs. V, calling for Pepe.

Mrs. V! I need to get to her. She would make things right. I slipped from the closet and grabbed my phone from my bed. I cracked my bedroom door and listened again. No singing. No heavy, negative feeling in the air. Nothing strange. I swung the door open and bolted. I ran down the hall, past the balcony, down the stairs.

When I neared the bottom step, my flip flop slipped off, and I stumbled, falling down the last four. I tried to grab the banister, but missed. My knee and shoulder took the brunt of the landing, skidding just a little on the carpet. I pushed myself up onto my hands and knees, hair hanging down around the sides of my face.

Singing drifted down the stairway. A clammy sweat broke out all over my body. *I've got to get out of here.* I struggled to my feet.

I ran out the front door, across the yard, and through Mrs. V's front door without knocking. I stood for a moment with my back against the door, trying to calm myself down. I'd never hyperventilated before, but I wondered if that was what was happening now.

Pepe ran from the bedroom, yipping and wagging his tail. "Mrs. V?" I called into the empty living room.

"Jenna? Dear, is that you?" Mrs. V asked from her bedroom. Was she taking a nap? I wondered.

"I'm so sorry, Mrs. V. I didn't mean to barge in, but I really need to talk to you again," I said. Now that I was safe, I bent over to look at my knee. Carpet burn. No blood. Shoulder. A little blood, but not much. I wasn't going to die.

I felt okay enough to take a seat on the same emerald green couch that I sat on yesterday. I chewed my lip and glanced around the room.

"What's wrong, dear?" Mrs. V asked. She emerged from her bedroom. Her hair was slightly messy on one side. I felt so bad for waking her up.

"I saw her again," I said. "I mean, I heard the ghost. I didn't really see her."

"What in heaven's name are you talking about?" she asked and sat next to me. Pepe jumped into my lap, obviously concerned. He wiggled his tail and licked at my chin. I pulled him close and hugged him for a moment. Mrs. V's hand smoothed my dark, tangled hair and patted my back before pulling her hand away. "Oh my, honey. You're sweating something terrible." Her voice took on a more concerned sound than yesterday, as if she realized this wasn't a one-time deal.

"Yesterday, I saw a little girl ghost at the top of the stairway," I said. "That's when I came over here. Now, this morning I was in my room, and I heard this weird singing out in the hallway. It had to be the ghost. I almost jumped out the window but was afraid I'd break my leg, so I hid in the closet." I looked at Mrs. V. "My house is haunted!"

Mrs. V took in a breath as if she were processing everything I told her. "Honey, we really need to talk with your mom about this."

"I can't."

"Why not?"

"Mom's in one of those moods again."

"Oh, dear," she said and paused for a moment. "Maybe I should go over and take a closer look."

"No!"

Mrs. V looked at me, her eyes full of love and worry. "We've got to do something, Jenna. This isn't healthy. If I go over there and don't see anything, will that make you feel better?"

"No."

"Why not?"

"It's scary. Just please don't go. Stay here with me—please," I said, but Mrs. V let out a sigh and stood. Pepe jumped from my lap. "What are you doing?" I asked and straightened.

Pepe barked while he made small circles. "Just stay here, dear," Mrs. V said. She and Pepe walked to the door. "I'm going to go take a look. I'll be right back."

The door clicked behind them. My nerves all jumped

at once. I remained on the couch, wishing for a cup of warm cocoa. A second later, the image of the ghost crawling out of my picture flashed in my mind. I shook my head.

If anyone had seen me, they probably would've thought I was a crazy person. Crazy? Maybe that's what was going on. I glanced at the door. *Where is Mrs. V? Wonder what's going on.* I bounced my knee and looked around her living room.

Pepe's sharp bark broke the silence. And not just one bark, a group of urgent barks. My heart jumped. The barks called for me, telling me something was wrong.

I stood and rushed through the door into the street. It only took a second before I stood at my own front door.

It stood open.

Mrs. V, in the middle of the living room, was on her knees. The ghost flew wildly around the open balcony space above, dipping and diving. My legs and knees weakened.

Mrs. V's hands came up to cover the sides of her head. She bent her head and curled into herself. I wanted to scream, but I couldn't. A cold wind picked up and whipped through the living room. Pepe ran back and forth, trying to chase the ghost off.

I wanted to turn and run away. But I couldn't leave Mrs. V. I just couldn't. I loved her too much. *I have to help her*! My legs didn't want to move, so I grabbed the door frame for stability and made myself take a step into the house. *I have to help her*! Once I was moving, I kept going and hurried to her side. I grabbed her shoulders.

"Come on, Mrs. V! Get up," I said and pulled. "We've got to get out of here." My hair blew from side to side with each pass of the ghost. A magazine flapped, pages flipping back and forth in the wild breeze that had taken over the living room. Mrs. V shifted her weight and tried to stand but then she started to sway. "Mrs. V?" I looked into her eyes, but she wasn't really looking back.

The sunlight filtered through the open door and mixed with the gray and white in her hair. I couldn't help but notice how she looked like an angel, glowing, frozen in time during one of the scariest moments of my life.

After staring at nothing for a few seconds, her eyes finally focused on me. Her lips moved a bit, as if she were trying to say something, but only a soft breath escaped. She tried again. "Dear…" she started. But then her eyes looked past me, no longer focused.

She swayed again. Losing all balance, she started to fall to the side. I wrapped my arms around her and lowered her gently to the floor. Pepe stopped barking. The wind stopped churning. The magazine stopped flapping.

And then the ghost disappeared.

CHAPTER 3

An hour later, Mom and I sat together in the waiting area of the St. Mary's Hospital emergency room. I'd called her right after the ambulance left, but I couldn't tell her what really happened. Not yet anyway. Did the ghost purposefully hurt Mrs. V? Or did Mrs. V have a heart attack or stroke because of being so scared? From what I'd seen, it looked like the ghost attacked her. And if the ghost had hurt Mrs. V, would it do the same to Mom? Tamara?

A wet nose nudged my forearm. Pepe. He fit perfectly in my school bag, so I'd brought him with us. I hoped that he'd help Mrs. V somehow. Maybe her love for him would pull her from the darkness.

"Jenna and Mrs. Moores? You can see her now," said a voice from behind us.

I turned. It was the doctor who was taking care of
Mrs. V, tall and dark with the most sincere look I'd ever
seen. Mom stood and waited for me. I gently pulled up
the sides around Pepe's nose and ears, so she couldn't see
him.

The emergency room bustled with activity, which
was the opposite of the calm of the waiting room. People
wearing scrubs came in and out of closed doors. Some
pushed curtains closed. Some stood behind the counter,
discussing important information with other people wearing scrubs. We followed Mrs. V's doctor into her room.

I wasn't sure what to expect. I wasn't even aware
that I held my breath. But when I saw the beeping machine attached to her arm and the thing stuck in her nose
to help her breathe, all the air I'd been holding whooshed
out of me. I grabbed the edge of the counter.

"Jenna, honey. What's wrong?"

Mom cradled my elbow and pushed my brown bangs
out of my eyes. I pulled away. Pepe whined in my book
bag. A plaguing voice went around and around in my
head. *This is your fault*! I shook my head as if that would
get rid of the voice.

"Why don't you sit down, sweetheart?" Mom guided
me to one of the chairs in the room, only I didn't want to
sit. I didn't want to be in the room anymore.

"I need some air," I managed to mumble and took off
through the door with Pepe held close to my chest. I
stumbled through the emergency room, vaguely aware of

the people around me. Only when I finally made it through the last set of doors and out into the late July summer day, did I finally slow down. Off to my left, bushes and a shallow recess in the side of the building offered a place to hide.

I sat with my legs crossed and Pepe in the bag on my lap. His nose poked out the top. "I'm so—so sorry."

My voice went up a notch, and my face scrunched. My stomach twisted and tightened even more. My shoulders shook. The tears spilled. Once I started, I couldn't stop. It turned into an uncontrollable moment fuelled by fear and guilt.

I sucked in shallow breath after shallow breath. A small wail escaped, and I pressed my hand over my mouth, afraid someone would hear, afraid they would know what really happened. Pepe scrambled from my bag to be by my side. He jumped and placed his paws on my shoulder, trying to get me to look at him. When I finally did, he licked the tears from my face.

After I'd cried all the tears I could, I swept my fingers underneath my eyes and took a deep breath of the hot afternoon heat. There was no hiding the fact that I'd been crying, but at least I could look a little more collected.

I scooped Pepe up, put him back in my bag, and carried him through the hospital doors. The air conditioning felt good after being outside in the late July heat. I peeled my shirt from my sticky skin, marched through the emergency room doors, and made my way to Mrs. V's room. When I walked in, Mom sat in the chair that she'd tried to get me to sit in. The doctor was gone.

The sight of Mrs. V lying there brought the tears to my eyes again, but I forged ahead. I went to her side and stood for a moment, hoping for some type of response or movement, something that said she knew I was there. When she didn't move, I pulled Pepe from the bag and held him to my chest.

I could feel him breathing against me. He softly whined and wiggled just a little like he wanted down, like he needed to check things out for himself. I let him down on the edge of the bed by her arm. He sniffed her shoulder and then sniffed her face. His whine became a little louder and a little more persistent.

Come on, Mrs. V, come back to us.

Pepe persisted with his own pleas. We stood there for a few minutes, Pepe and I, making our wishes known before Mom put her hand softly on my shoulder. "That's enough, honey."

I slipped my hand into Mrs. V's for a minute, gently squeezing it to let her know we were here. "I'll take care of Pepe, Mrs. V, until you get better and get out of here," I said before I let go of her hand.

Later that evening, they admitted Mrs. V to a room upstairs. The dark-haired doctor said that we'd just have to wait and see. All her signs and symptoms said she'd had a stroke.

ℰℐℰℐ

Pepe and I sat on the couch in Mrs. V's hospital room, a single patient room, small, yet cozy with a two-person tan couch. I wondered if the couch folded out for visitors that needed to stay the night.

The hospital had called her daughter, Mrs. V's emergency contact, as soon as she came in this morning. All of her family lived out of state. So I decided to stay until they got here. Mom didn't argue. She knew she couldn't win.

A chicken strip basket sat in front of me. Mom had gone down to the cafeteria to make sure I had something to eat in case I got hungry. I reached for a strip, broke off a piece, and offered it to Pepe. He turned his nose away. He wasn't hungry either.

I thought about how Mrs. V was like a grandma to me, maybe even closer. Ever since we moved next door to her, I spent every Christmas vacation with her. Mom and Dad usually had to work.

Mrs. V and I had so much fun. At first when I was younger, she came to my house, and we would play games until satisfied we'd played enough. I remember when her nephew gave Pepe to her. Only just a little guy, she brought him over so that I could play with him, too. Mrs. V confided in me that Pepe was the best Christmas gift she ever got.

When I got a little older, I would go to her house.

We spent time going through her family albums and going through all of her knickknacks on the living room shelves. Along with what seemed like hundreds of picture frames and small statues of every type of bird you could think of, she had one Precious Moments figurine.

The figurine was of a little girl snuggled up next to her grandma with a book in her lap. I remember how I would get so excited when the time came for her to explain who gave it to her. She would take it down and let me hold it. I would cup my other hand around it to keep it safe. Special to Mrs. V. And special to me. Because I had my own collection of Precious Moments figurines Dad had given me every year for my birthday. That was the main thing we had in common, our Precious Moments.

The door to Mrs. V's room opened and a nurse with glasses came in, smiled, and checked the numbers on the machine. I couldn't tell if she noticed Pepe curled up behind my legs, but I didn't care. He needed to be here with her just as much as I did.

After the nurse left, Pepe sighed and stretched his back legs. My phone beeped with a text from Tamara. *Coming over? Waiting!*

So much had happened that I forgot about making plans to lounge at the pool. *Sorry. Won't be able to make it* ☹.

I put my phone away, even though she'd texted back right away. I just couldn't tell her about Mrs. V or the ghost right now. I didn't have it in me. I reached over and ran my fingers over the black curls on Pepe's forehead. He tilted his head enough that he could meet my gaze. The lost look in his eyes broke my heart.

"Don't worry," I whispered, "everything will be okay." He blinked a few times and looked away.

⌒∂⌒∂

Once Mrs. V's daughter, Jessica, and her family arrived at the hospital, I called Mom to come and pick me and Pepe up. Jessica lived six hours away, near Cleveland, Ohio, and had three children of her own. I'd met them a few times. The nephew that had given Pepe to Mrs. V lived farther away. He would have to take a plane.

Jessica approached me, tears in her eyes, Kleenex in her hand. "Thanks for helping her, Jenna, and staying with her." She had swept her curly strawberry blonde hair up into a messy bun. Her lips were drawn tight. Her chin quivered.

Don't cry. Don't cry. I sucked in a deep breath and nodded, unable to meet her eyes. "If you want," I tried to say but the words were more of a croak. I cleared my throat. "If you want, I'll take care of Pepe."

"That will help a ton, at least for now." She pulled me close and gave me a hug. "We'll take him after we figure things out."

I nodded.

A little later, Mom pulled up in front of the hospital

entrance. Pepe and I climbed in the TrailBlazer. On our ride home, the sun sat low in the sky. Plenty of light still lingered in the late evening. I caressed Pepe's ears and silently reassured him that I would fix this. I was the one that got Mrs. V into this mess. I would be the one to get her out.

ငာသငာ

But before we made it home, Mom cleared her throat and adjusted her hands on the steering wheel. "Jenna, honey. There's something we need to talk about."

Too busy reassuring Pepe at first, I didn't answer. But when I finally looked at her, the passing background blurred, and I saw her more clearly—more clearly than I had this morning. Her shoulder-length brown hair hung limp, missing its normal curl at the end and her bangs were pulled back, secured with a bobby pin against the rest of hair. Normally they gracefully brushed her eyebrows. She was fighting her battle again. Maybe tomorrow would be better.

Lost in thought, I'd stopped rubbing Pepe's ears. His tiny paws danced on my lap, urging me to continue petting him. When I looked at Mom again, her bottom lip folded in and she chewed on it, waiting for me to say something.

Unsure of where she was going with this, I stayed silent.

She continued. "Honey, I know this is a bad time, but we need to talk about something." She squeezed the steering wheel. "Your dad and I talked and made some plans before he passed away." She waited a moment before going on. "We looked at other houses up north."

My head jerked back like she'd smacked me. "Why?"

"Because I'd like to be close to *my* mom and dad. The reason we moved here was because of your dad's job, and now that he's gone, there's no reason for us to stay—"

"What are you talking about? Of course there's a reason!"

"I know you're close to Mrs. V, but your own grandparents want to spend more time with you and get to know you better. We live too far away!" She smacked the steering wheel. Pepe let out a bark.

"We can't leave. I can't leave her like this!" I hadn't realized I'd stopped petting Pepe and had him close against my chest until he licked my cheek.

"I'm sorry, honey. If I'd known something like this was going to happen, we wouldn't have put an offer on that house." She reached over and patted my knee. "I just didn't think they would accept it so quick. I should've said something to you before now."

We were almost home. The evening sunlight flashed occasionally between the houses, blinding me from what was about to happen.

Mom sighed and her shoulders sagged. "I'm sorry. Really, honey. But we're supposed to close within the next month. You're going to have to start packing. It's not that far away and we can come back if Mrs. V needs us or something happens."

Or something happens.

My stomach twisted and I sank back against the car seat. I couldn't believe it. Mrs. V was in trouble. In trouble because of me, and now I was moving away. I hugged Pepe and smoothed his fur just how Mrs. V would smooth my hair if she were here.

CHAPTER 4

I was moving. I didn't want to leave, especially when Mrs. V and Pepe needed me. They needed me to find a way to destroy the ghost in the blue dress. Because if the ghost in the blue dress was responsible, destroying her would bring Mrs. V back.

That night after Mom went to bed, I pulled out my phone and started to text Tamara. My fingers hit button after button trying to explain a scary ghost, Mrs. V in the hospital, and moving. My heart sank. I didn't want to discuss it right now. I had to save Mrs. V.

I deleted the text and grabbed my laptop to research ghosts. After skimming multiple websites, I figured out that the ghost was tied to this world by something. A link of some sort.

In order to destroy it, I had to find and burn the link

that the ghost in the blue dress had to this world—before we moved.

The following evening, I sat alone in my room. Mom had gone to the store to get more moving supplies. I pushed the only box I'd packed into the corner and glanced around. Deep purple covered the previously pink walls that had had a princess border at the top. Posters replaced the white shelves. A yellowish-gold comforter with entwined roses embroidered throughout decorated my bed, given to me by Mrs. V on my thirteenth birthday. The room was empty, along with the rest of the house.

It was time.

I picked up Pepe and held him close, breathing in the scent of his shampoo and his freshly eaten doggy biscuit. Pepe's smell, his alone. I rubbed my cheek against his fur for a moment before sitting on the edge of the bed. I sat him next to me.

"Now listen, Pepe." His ears perked. "I have a big and dangerous job to do here. But I have to do it to save Mrs. V." He sat and cocked his head to the side, listening carefully. "I need you to stay here, okay?"

I stood and left Pepe sitting on the edge of the bed, ears still perked. I walked out of my room, closed the door, walked down the hall, the balcony on my right. I neared the top of the stairway. I paused for a moment, waiting, watching. I started down the steps, placing one barefoot at a time on the burgundy carpet, hand on the railing. The late July sun seeped in around the slats of the horizontal wood blinds, casting most of the living room in shadows.

I knew the ghost was here, by the stairway. I could feel her, that heavy feeling. The warm air, charged with negativity, settled on my skin as I made my way down. When I approached the bottom step, a quick gust of hot putrid-smelling air hit me from behind. My stomach lurched, not only from the smell that I could almost taste, but also from the fear that shot through my chest and shoulders like an arrow. I grabbed the railing with my other hand and held on tight.

After the gust had passed, I made it down the last two steps. I straightened and brushed my hair back from my forehead with trembling hands, some of the strands sticking to my sweaty fingers. Was that an attack? I grew anxious, worried about what else she would do. I turned to look at the top of the stairs, but they were empty.

The antique, walnut China cabinet sat against the wall off to the right. I'd helped Mom pack everything in it earlier, everything except one item. I walked over and squatted, opening the bottom door. There, where I had purposely left it, sat the picture of me at the age of four in a blue dress with white lace ruffles. Mom had it taken shortly after we'd moved in. Not long after that, during my first thunderstorm, I saw a little ghost with blonde hair crawl out of the picture frame and into the darkness.

This, I thought, *has to be the link.*

Even though I didn't want to touch it, I reached out.

My nerves pulsed and strained against my skin and an anxious feeling swelled within my chest. I pulled back and checked over my shoulder. The living room seemed darker now, more so than it should at this time of the evening.

Before I could convince myself to grab it and run, thunder quietly rumbled. Deep and angry and crackling with life. I hurried to the bay window and adjusted the blinds. The southwestern sky flashed violently, as if someone were flipping a light switch on and off.

Great. I needed to move or my plan would be ruined. I went back to the China cabinet and grabbed the picture. My heart drummed against my chest. Quickly, I shut the door and hurried to the kitchen. On the other side of the room was the door that connected the kitchen to the garage, and in the garage were a lighter and lighter fluid, the other two ingredients in my plan. A plan, I could tell, she didn't approve of, because when the air turned heavy and oppressive, I knew she was here.

ოოო

She appeared in the kitchen in front of the door I needed to go through. We faced each other like duelists, her spirit form faintly visible in the darkened kitchen. But I could see her smile, an evil menacing-type smile. A second later, as she continued to stare at me, her smile changed—no longer menacing but more loving.

She held out her hand to me. I stepped back, away from her invitation. But then it looked like her attention went to something behind me. I turned and glanced over my shoulder into the living room below the balcony. Nothing. When I turned back around—she was gone.

I stood with the picture in my hand, not sure of what had just happened. A light rain tapped on the kitchen window in a more steady rhythm, trying to bring me back to reality and make me remember my mission. My mission—to destroy her and save Mrs. V.

I continued through the kitchen and out into the garage. The lighter and starter fluid were in the back by the grill. I tucked the lighter fluid under my arm and picked up the lighter. I remembered Dad using it to light the grill, because the starter button no longer worked. I shook my head. No time for memories.

When I opened the side door of the garage and stepped outside, the late evening humidity enveloped me like a cocoon. I inhaled the smell of rain. The urgency of the approaching storm pushed me forward.

I turned and ran, almost tripping over my sandals as I made my way around to the back of the garage to the large trash bin. Once there, I paused for a second and looked at the picture. My breaths came quickly, not just from running but also from holding the picture frame. It seemed harmless now, but I knew what lurked inside. An old memory resurfaced, a memory of running down the stairs during my first thunderstorm and glancing up in time to see the ghost change my picture to a picture of her, unfold her hands from her lap, turn, and climb out of the picture.

I shuddered and dropped it, creating a small crack in the glass, but that wasn't good enough. I picked it up and threw it hard—so hard that the glass shattered. I grabbed the picture frame, shook the broken glass into the trash bin, and then dropped it back on the ground, exposing the picture of my innocent four-year-old face to the steam of lighter fluid that I poured all over it. The light sprinkle continued.

I have to hurry.

Once I saturated the picture, I clicked the lighter to life, lowering myself. I sat for a second, staring at the flame, as I slowly and carefully inched the lighter closer and closer to the oak frame.

Suddenly, I heard a girlish giggle behind me. My neck tingled, and I jerked my arm, pulling the flame away from the picture. I stood and searched the empty back-yard. The sound was so quiet, I almost talked myself into thinking it never happened. But I could feel her. I knew she was here.

I spun around and knelt to the ground. With my heart pounding, I quickly touched the flame to the picture and watched the fire spread—racing, glowing, dancing—from the image of my neatly folded hands in my lap to the bow in my light brown hair.

A second later, the fire let out a "wooomp," and I

watched the flames settle in to do what I needed them to do—destroy.

I stood. "Leave," I said in a firm, *I-mean-business* voice. "I am destroying any ties you have to this world." The fire crackled and burned hot with the accelerant.

But while I watched the flames fight the light sprinkling rain, a fear that I kept in the back of my mind started to surface. I pushed it back.

The flames pushed toward the edges of the picture and they began to curl. After a few seconds, the Trail-Blazer pulled into the driveway and into the garage.

No. Not yet. Not until I watched the picture burn and turn to ashes. Mom opened the door to the kitchen and called for me.

"Jenna? I've got pizza. Come help me with the boxes, honey," she said.

The picture was almost done burning anyway, but I still didn't want to leave. Smoke drifted and crackled upward against the soft sprinkling rain. If it were raining any harder, the fire wouldn't have survived. The burning picture gave off a sharp, smoky smell. I wanted to watch the fire burn totally out, but if I didn't go, Mom might come looking for me.

I turned and made my way back around to the front of the garage.

The wind blew a light sprinkle into the garage while I reached in and grabbed the extra moving boxes.

The smell of pizza lifted my mood along with the

image of dancing flames across the picture. Definitely ruined by now. Hopefully Mrs. V would be safe.

∽∾∽

That night, I slept. Restless, drifting in and out of awful nightmares, I kept dreaming that the ghost attacked Mrs. V. Stuck in the living room doorway looking in, I couldn't move. And when the ambulance showed up, they said she was dead. Then the police handcuffed me and took me to jail. But it was her hospital room instead.

The dream changed, and I was sitting on the couch, talking with her like nothing even happened, like she was herself again.

"It worked," she said. "I'm all better from the stroke."

Then I'd wake up and roll over. Pepe would whimper, stand, and do small circles before lying down again. Once I closed my eyes, another dream would come. Flames engulfed me, but I didn't feel them. I'd go along with my normal day, going to school, eating lunch all while burning.

Around midnight, I couldn't stand it anymore. I called the hospital. When a nurse answered I said, "I need to see how Mrs. Victoria Vanderley is doing." I heard some paper rustling through the phone. She asked my name. More paper rustling.

"Oh, yes. Jenna Moores. You're on the list here. Let

me see…" I closed my eyes and prayed, something I hadn't done much since Dad died. She had to be okay now. I just needed to know, so Pepe and I could get some sleep. "I'm afraid there's been no change," she said.

My stomach dropped and my chest tightened. "Wh— what?" I said, my voice hushed. "That can't be."

The nurse sighed. "I'm sorry." She sounded like she really meant it. "Maybe you should call back tomorrow and check again. Okay?"

I hung up the phone and looked at the clock. It'd been at least five hours since I'd burned the picture. I thought for sure she'd be okay by now.

I laid my head back against the soft pillow. After a moment, I reached into the top drawer of my nightstand and pulled out my sleep mask. I'd never really used it, but now seemed like a good time to try. I slipped it over my head and adjusted it against my closed eyes.

But I knew I still wouldn't sleep. And neither would Pepe, so he snuggled under the blanket, laid his chin on my shoulder, and whimpered. He let out a small frustrated sigh. I didn't bother to reassure him. He already knew.

CHAPTER 5

By the next afternoon, there was still no change in Mrs. V. The nurse at the hospital was tired of me calling. Mom was tired of me moping. And poor Pepe was just plain tired and lost. We clung to each other for support. We were the only ones that knew about the ghost. My phone beeped with messages from Tamara. Maybe I'd call her later.

I wasn't sure what to do now, to fix everything. I researched on the Internet everything I could about ghosts, and I still didn't know how to help Mrs. V. The picture was the only thing I knew of that could've been the link. I needed to get to the library and research this house.

"Library? We need to pack, honey," Mom said.

We stood in my parent's bedroom. I still considered it Dad's, too, even though he wasn't here, anymore.

Maybe that was another reason Mom wanted to move so soon.

I watched her wrap another picture frame in bubble wrap and lower it into a box. I looked around. It'd been only a few weeks since Dad had passed away. His stuff still hung in the closet. His computer desk was just as he left it. Dust covered the nightstand on his side of the bed.

"It's just for a little bit," I said softly. "I'll pack as soon as I get back. Please, Mom. It's really important."

She let out a breath and looked at me. Darkness hung under her eyes. "Just for an hour okay?" She glanced at the other side of the room where his computer desk sat. "I'm going to need your help," she said low and soft.

I pedaled the bicycle faster and faster. I hadn't ridden my bike for ages, but it was the quickest way to get to the library. Pepe's ears fluttered in the wind as he crouched in my bag. I wore my backpack on my front and rode with one hand, so I could keep an eye on him. At first, I'd gone slow, afraid he'd jump out, but he didn't. He knew we were on a mission, so I picked up the pace. Before long, we were pulling up in front of the library on Meridian Street.

Pepe's nose stuck out of my bag as I carried him in. I found a computer catalog with no one near, so I could place him next to me. "Now," I whispered, "let's see what we can find."

First, I typed our address into the search bar and hit Enter. A few hits popped up but they were street maps and general information books about the town. Next, I typed in haunted house in Indianapolis. Multiple hits popped up, including something that looked interesting. I needed to go into the genealogy section of the library to find the book listed, so I wrote down the number.

I carried Pepe through the library and was just about to open the door to the genealogy section when I heard a familiar voice. "Jenna?"

I turned around. "Oh—hey, Tamara."

"What's going on? First, you blow me off, and now you're not returning my texts?" she asked with one fist on her hip and a book cradled in her other arm, auburn ponytail hanging over her shoulder. Her bright blue eyes flashed.

"I'm sorry," I said and shrugged. "It's been a bad couple of days. I'm not even sure I've checked my phone." My voice cracked a little.

"What's going on?" she asked again. Her eyes took on a softer look.

I sighed. I wanted to tell her everything, especially about the ghost. But I knew I shouldn't. Not until I knew what was going on. So I told her what I could. "Mrs. V had a stroke."

Her hand came up to her chest. "I'm so sorry, Jenna," she said in a soft voice. Her lips formed a straight line, and she shook her head. "I didn't know. I should've known something was wrong."

My eyes watered, and I looked away. During summer vacation, Tamara and I would go over to Mrs. V's a few times to play cards when we were bored, so she knew how much I cared for Mrs. V.

Tamara stepped closer. She smelled of coconut suntan lotion. "This just sucks. People *do* recover from strokes, though. Did they say anything about that?"

"Not really," I said. I had the eye watering under control now. "The doctor said we just have to wait and see." Pepe whined and shifted his weight in my bag. Tamara leaned over and peeked inside.

"Aaaahhh—poor Pepe," she said and rubbed his ear.

I sighed. "I know. Poor little guy. He's so lost without her." I adjusted the bag so he seemed more comfortable.

She stepped back. "Call me, okay? We can go to the movies or something. Get your mind off of everything."

"Sure," I said. "But I've got something else to tell you."

She paused. My eyes watered again. I didn't want to say it now. What if I cried in the middle of the library? I swallowed the lump and looked down.

"What is it, Jenna?" Tamara asked in a hushed voice.

"Never mind," I said. "I'll call you later."

Of course I wanted to tell her that I was moving, but if I did, I was going to cry. And not just any cry. I was about to have a breakdown. But I can't do that now. I needed to help Mrs. V and get things straightened out. I glanced in the direction I needed to go.

"I'd better get my stuff done. Mom'll be calling me to come home."

"Okay," she said. "But call me. Seriously. When you get home." She raised her eyebrows and gave me a look before she left, leaving a hint of coconut tanning lotion.

I blinked back the tears and took a deep breath. Pepe and I continued into the genealogy section. I set my bag down on a chair and let Pepe get comfortable before I left. I picked up the book I needed, returned to the table, and started thumbing through the pages, reading the news of what happened week to week. Nothing.

I flipped to the back and scanned the index. There had to be something here, something that would give me some insight into the ghost. Finally, I read the words "child dies." I flipped to the page. There were no pictures, but there was a copy of a small newspaper clipping. "Child Dies After Ingesting Poison."

I read the article. A sister handed her thirsty sibling a glass of liquid from the kitchen counter thinking it was water. But it wasn't. She died the next day.

I paged through the rest of the book. No other information popped out at me or looked like it would be useful. I closed the book and put it back on the shelf. Should I look anywhere else? I needed to find more than this. I ripped the falling ponytail holder from my dark hair and pulled my hair back up. I chewed my fingernail and considered going back to the catalog for another search when my cell phone beeped.

A text from Mom. She needed me to come home.

∽∾∽∾

I helped Mom pack Dad's things. Cardboard boxes filled slowly as I held up each article of clothing for Mom before packing it away. The sweater she'd bought him for his last Christmas brought her to tears. When she'd given it to him, cancer was just something scary that affected other people, other families. Not us. Five months later, Dad was gone.

That evening, I called the hospital again. The nurse had finally lost her sympathy for me. Mrs. V was still admitted and her doctor was talking to Mrs. V's family about putting her in a nursing home already.

I sat in my room on my bed. I'd just packed my cherry curio cabinet. It now stood bare with the last of my Precious Moments in a box, taped shut, with the word *FRAGILE!* written in black marker so that the movers would be careful. Dad had bought one every year for my birthday. So far, I had fifteen figurines.

I sighed, flopped down on my full-sized bed, and stared at the ceiling, thinking, worrying. Pepe jumped up beside me. I stroked his satiny ears. Dad was gone. Mrs. V was soon to be in a nursing home. Stroke they said. I couldn't talk to Mom. I just couldn't. What if the ghost hurt her, too? Then I thought of Tamara and how I wanted to tell her. I just wasn't sure what was going on yet. I didn't want to take the chance of someone else getting hurt.

I was alone.

Alone against the ghost.

I traced the stitching in my quilt that Mrs. V had given me—a beautiful yellow-gold satin with embroidered roses throughout. I'd painted my room a deep purple just to go with it.

I slowly followed its pattern as my mind turned from the ghost to Mrs. V. Even though we weren't related, she treated me like one of her own. She'd never missed grandparent's day at school. She'd never missed my birthday. But more than that, she could always tell when something was wrong. My eyes blurred with tears.

Dang it. I was going to cry again. What I would give to go back, to not involve her at all. What I would give to have a normal life again.

I sniffed and wiped at my eyes. I rolled onto my side and looked at the clock. Pepe hopped over my legs and came up next to me. I wrapped him in a hug. The sun had finally set, so I knew it was late. I sat up and grabbed my hair tie from the nightstand. Once I tied my long hair up into a ponytail, I changed into my nightgown.

I stood, went to my closet, and rummaged in the back. Shoes and clothes covered the box I needed.

With the top finally open, I grabbed my old teddy bear, Roscoe, and my worn pink baby blanket. It wasn't just a baby blanket, it was a security blanket, too. I closed the top and pushed the box back into the corner. I pulled the yellow-gold quilt back and tucked my pink blanket underneath. Maybe fifteen was a little old to need reassurance, but at this point, I didn't care.

My pink blanket, worn thin, had holes threatening to emerge at any time. I reached over and switched off my teardrop chandelier lamp and pulled Roscoe close with Pepe curled by my side. I started to close my eyes, but then realized I had forgotten something.

I reached under my pillow and found my sleep mask just as my phone beeped. A text from Tamara. I was going to have to tell her about me moving and soon. Half my room was already packed. I shut off my phone and pulled my sleep mask over my eyes. It was velvety against my eyes and face. Reassuring.

It reassured me that even if I felt the ghost's presence, I wouldn't see her. And if I didn't see her, maybe she really didn't exist.

⋐⋑⋐⋑

Monday. Trash day. Mom had left for work earlier, and it was my job to get the trash ready and get it to the curb. Only one thing slowed me down. The burned picture. Stupid and dangerous, I'd left it out there for the last couple of days, but I didn't want to go near it. Even though it wasn't the link to destroy her, she had possessed it at one time. And I'd never forget it.

Pepe and I went out the front door to enjoy a little of the morning. Plus he needed to do his business. Before coming in, he went over to Mrs. V's front door and sniffed. I was guessing he checked for her scent. My heart hurt for him. It really did.

I'd known Pepe his whole life and not once had Mrs. V left him. When she went to visit her family, Pepe went with her. I missed Mrs. V terribly. There was no way I could imagine how much Pepe missed her.

"Come on, little guy, let's get back inside." I opened the front door. He took his time walking in. I understood that the house spooked him. It spooked me too.

After I gathered all of the trash, I set it outside the open overhead garage door. I stood for a moment, waiting, not wanting to go back behind the garage. But I had to. The pickup truck would be here soon. I'd left Pepe inside, and I could hear him scratching and whining at the door.

"Don't worry, Pepe. I'll be right back."

He barked in return.

I took a deep breath and squared my shoulders. *I can do this.* I turned and walked between the garage and the neighbor's fence, making my way to the backyard to the trash bin and picture.

Even though the morning air was mild, sweat formed in my palms and under my arms. A nervous chill crawled across my body. I rounded the last corner, eyes glued to the ground.

When the picture frame came into view, my feet stopped.

I couldn't believe what I saw. How could this be? The edges of the picture were curled and charred, but the center of the picture was empty as if the photographer clicked the button without me being there.

The nervous chill crawled across my body and bit me, causing an intense numbing feeling to spread like venom. No little girl looked back at me from within the confines of the four sides of wood. A nauseous wave swept through me, and I sat down, cradling my legs to my chest.

I was not sure how long I sat there, but I almost missed the trash truck. Its rumbling start and the squeal of brakes came down our street, making its way slowly toward me, only a few houses away now. I had to get up.

After the numbness faded enough that I could feel my limbs, I swallowed the bile that rested in the back of my throat and stood. I looked at the empty picture frame again, not sure if I should leave it or throw it in the trash.

How could it be empty—I mean literally empty—and not be the link?

Even though the picture frame repulsed me, I was afraid to throw it away. I needed to know more before I did something like that. So, I left it where it lay and grabbed the trash bin, rolling it to the sidewalk just in time.

CHAPTER 6

The next day, Pepe and I went to the library again while Mom worked. There had to be something there. There had to be something to help me figure out how to destroy the ghost.

We sat at the same computer catalog as we did Saturday, at the end of the table, where someone would be less likely to notice Pepe. I searched my address again. A few hits popped up for zoning records or something of the sort.

Next search, "Ghosts in Indianapolis." A bunch of hits popped up. Scrolling down, I searched for something relevant, something that would make sense. I scrolled past a tag that said "Haunted Historic Theater."

That was new. I never knew that we had a haunted theater.

At that time, my momentum slowed and my high hopes started to fall. Who was I kidding? It was not like the answer was going to jump out at me. The thought that I might not find an answer and that I might not be able to save Mrs. V crept into the back of my mind. My hopes crashed to the floor.

I needed to think about the fact that I might not be able to save her. I continued to scroll through the library catalog, not ready to give up, picking up any pieces of hope I could find.

An hour later, no luck. Mom would be at work until evening, so I texted Tamara about coming over. I closed out of all my searches and tucked Pepe into my backpack to bike to Tamara's house.

Once I arrived, I knocked on her door.

Tamara opened it. "Jenna!" she said and let me in. Fresh from the pool, she stood in her bikini with a towel around her chest. "It's about time. How's Mrs. V?"

I shrugged. "No change. They're sending her to a nursing home."

"Oh."

"Yea," I said and sighed.

"Did you bring your bikini?"

"No. I can't stay. I didn't bring Pepe's food or anything. Plus, I didn't tell Mom I was coming over."

"Okay," she said. Her voice held a questioning tone.

"Look, I didn't plan today very well. A lot of things have been going on, but I've got some bad news."

Tamara cocked her head. "Spill it, Jenna. Come on. What's been going on?"

"I'm moving."

೮⁄つ೮⁄つ

Two days had passed and nothing had happened. I scraped my plate and put it in the dishwasher. No improvement in Mrs. V and no sign of the ghost in the blue dress. I had no leads or ideas of how to get rid of the ghost. I was starting to go crazy. I needed to get out. "Can we go to the hospital?" I asked.

I thought for sure Mom would say no to my whiney tone, but instead she scooted her chair back and stood. "Sure, honey." She held my gaze for a moment, and I knew her sadness had disappeared for now. "Maybe we can get ice cream, too."

That is unexpected, I thought and put her plate in the dishwasher. When I straightened, Mom was there, next to me. She opened her arms for a hug. We wrapped our arms around each other. At fifteen, I stood just a little taller than she, but I still laid my cheek against her shoulder, like I always did as a kid.

We clung to each other, swaying. The thought of losing her, too, caused a sharp jab of pain in the bottom of my stomach. I hugged her tighter.

Afterward, without any spoken words, we climbed into the TrailBlazer and started for the hospital. Pepe sat

on my lap, facing the air vents. He seemed to like the air
blowing in his face. And he seemed to know we were going to see Mrs. V.

Once we were there, he hid in my bag during our
trek through the halls and up the elevator. I smelled cafeteria food when the doors opened. Stainless steel carts sat
outside most of the rooms—except for Mrs. V's.

Even though I'd asked to come see her, an enormous
weight sat on my chest, and I couldn't breathe very well.
The weight, I realized, was the fact that I hadn't fixed
things yet. She should've been okay by now.

But she wasn't.

Mom knocked softly on the door before we walked
in. Her nephew, Steven, sat on the couch with his laptop.
His dark glasses looked professional against his blonde
hair. He had the same smile as Mrs. V.

"Jenna. How are you?" He came over and shook my
hand as if I were a celebrity. To him, I was the girl that
called the ambulance and saved his mom. Pepe squirmed
and let out a small bark at the sound of his voice. "Pepe!"
Steven leaned over, peered into my bag, and laughed. "I
can't believe you snuck him in here."

"Oh, he goes everywhere with me. I'm taking good
care of him." I reached in, gently scooped him up, and
handed him to Steven.

After a moment, I finally looked at Mrs. V. A plastic
tube was strung across her face and into her nose. A bag
full of liquid dripped into the IV attached to her arm. A

beeping machine stood next to it with numbers flashing.

The enormous weight on my chest seemed a little heavier and my breathing seemed more difficult. I had to sit.

Mom and Steven talked about the tragic stroke. He mentioned how sorry he was to hear about Dad—how you just never knew.

You just never knew.

The words tumbled through my head like a bad word game. You just never knew when your entire life was going to be ruined.

℘℘℘

Later that evening, after we left the hospital, Mom stopped for ice cream. I didn't feel like it, but she bought me my favorite anyway, chocolate strawberry soft swirl in a waffle cone. Nothing like a sugar rush when you were depressed.

She pulled the TrailBlazer over to a shady spot beside the gas station, rolled down the windows, and turned it off.

After she took a bite of her butter pecan cone, she pulled her knees up and shifted in her seat to face me. "Honey, we need to talk about a few things."

Pepe had jumped to the back seat and had his head out the window, smelling all of the new scents in the air. Mom had only cracked the back windows, afraid he might jump out if he saw something good enough to chase.

Remembering the hug earlier, I knew this was going to get deep, and I wasn't sure I could handle deep right now. I felt totally drained of emotions. Three months ago, I lost my Dad, and not even a week ago, I lost Mrs. V— two out of three of the most important people in my life. And Mrs. V's tragedy was my fault. If I hadn't asked her for help, she would be okay and not lying unconscious in a hospital room. I never should've let her go over there. I knew the ghost was real. I just never should've let her go.

"Honey?"

I turned to face Mom. "What?"

"Nothing. You looked like you were a mile away there for a minute." She reached over and squeezed my arm.

The look in her eyes hurt. She needed to talk. She needed closeness. She needed her daughter right now. "Sorry. Just thinking about Mrs. V."

"I know, honey. I know."

"So what did you want to talk about?" I asked. Melted ice cream flowed across my fingers. Even though I didn't feel like it, I ate a bite and wiped my fingers.

Mom sighed, a big *my-heart-is-hurting* sigh. "I love you, honey. And I can tell that you don't want to move. I understand, but that house holds too many memories for me…and you. Especially you, seeing poor Mrs. V suffer a stroke in the living room. Just think about it." She adjusted her leg and looked almost excited for a moment. "We'll have a new place to make new memories. I'm not saying to forget, just to—" Her gaze upward for a moment before she found her words. "—move on."

This was the most excitement I'd seen from her in months. I smiled. I smiled for her because she needed it, because she wanted it, and because her emotional state depended on it.

"I get it." I nodded. "I'm with you, Mom. Don't worry."

I could see the tears building and reflecting even though we were in the shade. "Did I tell you it's in the country?" I shook my head. "Did I tell you it has a barn?"

"Noooo."

"Did I tell you it has a pasture big enough for a couple of horses?"

At that, I felt a lightness in my chest. "Noooo." A horse? I'd always wanted a horse. For that single moment, I let the lightness fill my chest completely, so completely it pushed all of the darkness out.

"Sooooo." Mom drew out the word like an excited teenager and swiped her bangs to the side. "What do you think?" Her eyes were wide, waiting for me to respond.

I sucked in a breath and said, "Great! A horse would be great!"

"I knew it!" She squeezed my arm again and took another bite of her cone. "I knew it," she said again, more to herself than to me.

She started the engine and pulled out of the shade into the sunlight.

Pepe jumped to the front to ride in my lap. I held onto the lightness in my chest, savoring it. It'd been too long since I'd felt this way, and I knew it wouldn't last for long.

CHAPTER 7

The following week, Jessica and her family moved Mrs. V to a nursing home near Cleveland, Ohio. They were going to get her situated and then come back for Pepe. I think they felt bad for me and wanted to let me keep him a little longer. I wanted to keep him forever.

But I knew that wasn't right. He should be with his family. I just felt like we supported each other and once that support was gone, I would be totally alone. Pepe was the only one that knew and really understood.

Throughout the following week, Pepe and I spent most of our days at Mrs. V's house, cuddling on the couch or lounging in the backyard. That way, Pepe felt more at home, and we weren't as afraid of the ghost.

Each day, we would eat lunch and then take a nap.

When we woke, we went back outside and played fetch and then lay in the sun and napped some more. Along the way, I cleaned his bed and his food and water bowl. I packed some of his things that we didn't use every day like his stuffed toys and shampoo and brush, so they were ready when Jessica came to pick him up.

By Thursday afternoon, I had a tan and Pepe looked a little slimmer from all the fetch games we'd played. And tomorrow, it was all going to end.

ფოჟ

Friday morning, I woke, stretched, and reached out to find Pepe, but he wasn't there. I sat up and glanced around my room, but he wasn't there either.

"Pepe?" Maybe he needed to go out and Mom had taken him. I climbed out of bed and went to my door. It was cracked just enough for a little poodle to get through. I opened it and peered down the hall to the balcony.

There he sat, completely still. I walked out of my room and started down the hall. This wasn't normal. The back of my neck tingled. The heaviness in the air increased the closer I got to the stairs and the closer I got to him.

"Pepe," I whispered. He whined, wagged his tail a few times, and then fell silent. Panic rose in the pit of my stomach. But, along with the panic rose, a strong urge to protect him.

I broke into a run. I ran the rest of the way down the hall and onto the balcony. Without losing too much speed, I reached down and scooped him up. I ran down the stairs and out the front door, holding him close. Once we made it to Mrs. V's house, I set him down.

"Pepe?" I got down on all fours and peered into his dark eyes. "Pepe, are you okay?"

He let out a low growl and looked around the living room. Then he went from the TV stand to the other corner of the living room, sniffing and growling, until he felt content that the ghost wasn't here.

He came up to me, placed his paws on my shoulder, and let out a small whine.

I touched my forehead to his. "I know, boy. I know. There's a ghost in the house, and I know things are dangerous. That's why I know you need to go with Aunt Jessica even though I want you to stay with me."

My heart ached. I didn't want him to leave. But I couldn't be selfish right now. "I know you'll have fun at Jessica's. They'll take good care of you." My heart ached some more. Not only had my world been turned upside down but so had his.

We lay on the couch and turned on the TV. He jumped up beside me and curled himself behind my legs. Occasionally I could feel him growl. Then I'd stroke his ears and back. The growling would stop, only to start up again an hour later. Poor Pepe.

Friday went by so slow, I couldn't stand it. I never

considered the fact that the ghost might hurt Pepe. And now I wanted him to leave and be safe.

That evening, Jessica pulled up in front of my house. I'd been watching for her, so when I stepped out of Mrs. V's front door, she looked a little confused.

"Are those pajamas?" She and her kids walked into Mrs. V's house, and I closed the door.

I looked down at my clothes. "Oh, yeah. I decided to help pack Pepe's things this morning. We ended up watching some TV, and I forgot to change." I shrugged, the only excuse I could think of last minute.

The kids ran to the couch and took turns petting Pepe. He wagged his tail and seemed to forget about the ghost for a moment.

I motioned to a box that had all of his things in it. "I guess we need to empty his food and water bowl now." I went to the kitchen and grabbed the last of his stuff, including his dog food. "This is the only food he likes," I said and put it in the box. "Don't waste your money on anything else." I folded the flap over, tucked it underneath the other, and paused for a moment. Earlier in the week, I'd packed some of my boxes to move and now I was packing Pepe's box. I let out a slow sigh and straightened.

"Let me grab that," Jessica said and picked up the box.

She turned toward the door. I opened it for her to carry the box to the van. When I turned back around, one of the younger kids was running with Pepe right behind her. One of the older kids whistled for him and held out a treat. Pepe took it gently from his hands and crunched away on it, finishing it within a few seconds. He sniffed for more.

My eyes started to fill, but I took a deep breath. This is the only way—the only way for Pepe to be safe.

When Jessica came back in, she called for the kids to get in the van and get ready. Then she turned to me. "I don't know how to thank you, Jenna. You've been such a help."

"No problem," I said and smiled, hoping she couldn't see through the smile, hoping she couldn't see through the lie. "He's the best. I hope it's all right if I come and visit him and Mrs. V." The last few words came out with a little more emotion than I intended, so I smiled again.

Jessica nodded and then wrapped me in her arms. "You bet, kiddo. Please come when you can."

We walked outside into the evening and closed the door. Jessica probably figured I'd go back to my house. With four happy kids and a little barking dog, Jessica started the van and drove slowly by so everyone could wave goodbye. Pepe barked—sharp, frantic, worried.

When they had turned the corner and couldn't see me anymore, I fell to the step, buried my head in my knees, and sobbed and sobbed and sobbed. Once I had cried myself out, I glanced up and down the street, taking in the neighborhood from Mrs. V's front step. *This will be the last time I sit here. This will be the last time in her house since Jessica took the key.*

After a few minutes of deliberating, going from feeling guilty to knowing Mrs. V would want me to have it, I stood and walked back into her house and carefully took her Precious Moments from the shelf.

ややや

The following week whizzed by in a blur of packing and phone calls. I finally called a few other friends and told them that I was moving. Tamara had talked with most of them. We decided to get together Wednesday afternoon at her pool and finish with pizza and ice cream that evening. This was the last week in the house, and I had no idea how to destroy the ghost and save Mrs. V.

By this time, I'd accepted that I wasn't going to be able to save her. I didn't know how, and nothing at the library helped. By this time, I was just frustrated and wanted to leave everything behind. And I felt terrible about it.

When Wednesday afternoon rolled around, I changed into my turquoise bathing suit and sat on the edge of the bed where Pepe and I had just sat a week ago. I missed his little barks and his wagging tail and his doggy scent. I'd called Jessica Monday morning, and she said he was doing fine, moping around a little, probably missing me. I couldn't stop the lump from forming in my throat. I missed him, too. I grabbed my bag, phone, and flip flops and headed down stairs to meet my friends and say good-bye.

CHAPTER 8

Thursday and Friday blurred together, and I was more than happy for the distraction of packing and cleaning. Less time to worry. When I woke Saturday morning, I watched the sun filter through the blinds of the curtain-free window throwing a dark, light, dark, light pattern across the opposite wall. I knew that if I lay there another hour the pattern would eventually crawl across my floor to my bed where Pepe used to sleep.

After my shower, I twisted my hair into a knot on the top of my head, ready for the two-hour drive. I finished packing my comforters, gently folding the pink one and laying it on top.

Then I pulled out my teddy bear, Roscoe. His eyes still held the promise of love and safety and his worn nose still had a small piece of velvet. I placed him on top and fluffed the comforter around him, so he would be well protected during the move. I closed the box and taped it shut. After a moment, I grabbed the black marker and wrote *FRAGILE!* on top.

A knock sounded at my bedroom door. I turned to see Mom. Her shoulder length hair, a little darker than mine, hung gracefully around her face. She smiled, a genuine smile that reached her eyes and radiated throughout her body.

"Are you about ready?" she asked.

I nodded. "Yep. Can't wait."

My cheery tone didn't fit my mood. A heavy weight had plopped into the bottom of my stomach at the thought of Mrs. V. Here I was getting ready to leave her behind, more like abandon her. I had asked her for help, and now I was leaving her.

"Me, too." Mom's smile faded. "Seems awful quiet doesn't it?" she said and looked around my room. She shook her head. "Anyway—meet me downstairs when you're ready."

The door closed softly. The room seemed like a vacuum. If I screamed I wouldn't be able to hear myself, like a black hole except on earth and in my room. After a final look around, I grabbed my overnight bag and walked to my bedroom door.

When I opened it, the vacuum disappeared and sound filled my room. Birds chirped. Cars drove up and down the streets. The neighbor's dog barked. I closed the door.

Silence.

The fear that I had pushed back the night when I burned the picture sprouted. I opened the door and hurried down the hall to the stairs. I jumped down the last two steps, causing my bag to fall from my shoulder.

Mom glanced up from the living room couch. "What in heaven's name?"

I froze for a second, took a deep breath, and chanced a look up the stairway.

Nothing. No foul-smelling hot air or some strange vacuum. And definitely no spirit standing at the top of the stairs.

"Oh, I'm just really excited," I said casually. I put one hand on my hip and used the other to adjust my yellow tank top strap, which had slid off my shoulder.

"You act like someone lit a fire under your butt," she said and shook her head.

If only you knew.

"I just finished packing the kitchen," Mom added. "Other than that, I think we're ready."

"Sounds good to me," I said.

"I'm going to check all the rooms one last time."

I nodded and headed for the kitchen door. "I'll throw my bag in the backseat and wait on you out there."

യായ

After I stuffed my bag behind my seat and made sure

my CDs and iPod were accessible, I decided to take one last look at the picture frame. Uneasy about the episode in my room, I made my way around the side of the garage. I had to see the picture frame one more time before I left.

But before I made it to the trash can and before I could see the picture frame, I heard a noise, the squeak of a chain on a swing. Only we didn't have a swing set. An eerie feeling crawled over my body, like snakes slithering over my skin.

I shivered.

The air became heavy and the atmosphere depressing. I glanced around. The backyard remained empty except for a patio table that we never used anymore. The sound of the squeaking chain continued.

Giggling. A small child's voice called out. It sounded like the voice said, "Sissy."

I stood at the edge of the garage, watching our empty backyard, knowing it wasn't really empty.

I stood there for only a minute or so before I turned around and walked away. I didn't care about seeing the picture frame anymore. I knew it didn't matter. She was still here.

The kitchen door slammed. "Jenna! Where are you, honey?" Mom called.

"Here, Mom. I'm ready." I climbed into the Trail-Blazer.

"You don't look well," she said and felt my forehead.

I shook my head and looked out the window. "I'm fine."

She sighed and started the engine. "Not forgetting anything?"

"No."

"Okay," she said and put the truck in drive. "But I still feel like we're forgetting something."

CHAPTER 9

I turned up the volume on my iPod while my excitement faded. I chewed the side of my cheek and rocked my sandal-clad foot back and forth. Maybe there wouldn't be anything to worry about in the new house. Maybe we would start a new life with new memories like Mom said.

Maybe the sting of leaving Mrs. V in the nursing home would lessen.

The bright sun, only hidden for a few short minutes here and there by sparse clouds, warmed my skin. My brown tortoise-shell sunglasses blocked out most of it. Out of the corner of my eye, I saw Mom's lips forming words I couldn't hear. I silenced the latest from Beyoncé.

"Did you hear me?" Mom asked and raised her eyebrows. I shook my head. "I said do you want to stop for lunch in this next town. It's only a couple of miles so we need to decide."

"Sure," I said.

After lunch and miles away from the interstate, we drove north into the country. We drove in comfortable silence, both of us taking in the corn and soybean fields. After living in town for so long, I wasn't sure I could handle all of the openness here in Kayville, Indiana. Houses were spaced apart, anywhere from half a mile to a mile, with scattered wood clusters back behind them, like everyone had their own piece of woodland.

We slowed. She flipped her turn signal and turned right onto a dirt road. She gave me that smile, and I knew we were almost there.

After a quarter of a mile of cornfields on both sides, the TrailBlazer slowed to a crawl.

"It's on the left," she said. Then, as the corn stopped, a yard and driveway came into view before the small ranch-style house. I sat up and craned my neck. Then I saw it. A small red barn sat in the back left corner with a hayfield rolling in the background. We turned into the small white gravel driveway, and she turned off the truck, sitting in silence for a few seconds.

The silence killed me, and I couldn't help but ask, "When are we getting horses?"

She sighed. "I have to take care of a few things first."

"Like...what kind of things?"

"It's going to take more money than I thought to fix

the fence. I just got a quote last night. But don't worry, sweetheart, it won't be long."

I sank back into my seat, and so did my heart. The only thing that I really looked forward to was now gone. When Mom talked about money, it would take awhile. I swallowed the lump that had formed in my throat and pulled myself slowly from the TrailBlazer, all excitement gone.

The barn sat on the west side of the house. When I approached, I could see that Mom was right. The fence needed a lot of work. Replaced would be more like it. I wiped at a tear that had slipped below my sunglasses.

I opened the side door and stepped in. Hot, humid, and musty. From the outside, the barn looked way too small to hold a horse and hay. But from the inside, the early afternoon sun cast enough light to see that it was a decent size. I pictured my horse, a palomino, standing in a stall. The saddle and bridle on the far wall. Hay in the corner.

"The house is unlocked now so you can see your new room." Mom walked up beside me and gave me a squeeze. "Maybe we could fit two horses in here. What do you think?"

"That would be great," I said and rested my head on the crook of her shoulder. I knew this wasn't her fault. She gave me a final squeeze, and we turned toward the house.

"Now here's the kitchen."

Mom ran her finger along the edge of the counter. We moved on in search of the other rooms. Her room sat at the end of one hall and mine at the other. But when she opened the door to my room, my jaw dropped.

"Pink? You have *got* to be kidding me."

And not just any pink—the exact shade of my old room before I painted it. The stuffiness of the room suffocated me. It seemed worse in here than in the barn.

"It's not a big deal. They had a little girl, too, and apparently this happened to be a popular shade." She swiped her bangs out of her eyes and crossed her arms. "The movers will be here in a few hours, and we'll just go back into town to get the paint. I can't remember everything." She let out a small laugh.

The stuffiness in the room pushed down on me, trying to fill my lungs. I couldn't breathe. The fear, guilt, and aggravation of the last month swirled around my head, amplified by the inability to take in a deep, cleansing breath. I circled the room and now stood by the closet. The feelings built, built, built until I had to do something to get rid of them. So I shoved the closet door. It slammed into the other side, making a loud banging sound that echoed throughout the empty room.

Mom jumped and turned to stare at me. The surprised look on her face hurt. I'd scared her. What was wrong with me?

"I'm sorry, Mom," I said, but I couldn't meet her eyes. The awful feelings were still there. Shoving the closet door didn't help. I needed to get out. I started for the bedroom door. "I don't know what got into me," I said, rushing by her and out of the room.

I'd never acted like that before in my life—all because my room was pink. It took me back to when I was four. Just like when I first saw the ghost.

CHAPTER 10

After we drove back into town in silence, we stopped at the paint store.

"May I help you?" a lady with a white vest asked.

"I wish you could," I said.

"I'm sorry?"

"I can't decide what color to paint my room," I said while I perused the color cards, getting drawn back to the same color each time.

"I see you like purple. That's a very sophisticated color for a young lady. Good choice," she said, shaking her head in exaggerated agreement.

"That's the color I had before. I want a change, but I don't really like anything else. Plus, it matches my bedspread."

"Oh? And what color is that?"

"Kind of a golden yellow with roses embroidered on it. It was a gift."

The sales woman gave me a slow smile. "Well, I'm sure they're delighted you like their gift."

"Do you have any idea of something different I could do?" I shuffled through a few different shades of purple, drawn to the darker, deeper tones.

The sales lady walked over to the wallpaper borders. "You could paint the bottom of the room dark purple and the top ivory then put one of these up. Or you could have an accent wall where you paint one wall purple then the other walls a lighter shade."

"Cool. I like that idea."

She smiled, pleased with herself. While she mixed up the colors I had picked out, I roamed the aisles of the store. The evening sun came in through the large windows overlooking the street. The faded hardwood floors creaked as I walked over and looked out. There were a few scattered people out on the sidewalk, taking their time visiting the ice cream shop and antique shop.

I turned to check out the other direction and caught sight of Mom walking out of the gas station across the street talking with someone.

A man. A man that climbed into a big truck hauling a horse trailer.

I hurried back to the paint counter just as the sales lady finished up. I shifted my weight back and forth, waiting on her to give me a total. She threw in the rollers and pan, things I knew I needed but had forgotten.

"Now I hope you like your new room," she said and handed me the bag.

"Thank you," I said and smiled. "By the way, are you hiring? I need a job." The idea sprang from the back of my mind. If I could earn enough money, I could help pay for the horse fence.

"We're not, but the Pizza Shop across the street is. They had a sign out just this afternoon."

I thanked her again and headed for the door just as Mom walked in. In my rush to see what she had to say, I tripped over the toe of my sandal. Luckily, I caught my balance by grabbing onto a nearby end cap instead of hitting the floor.

Only a few cans of spray paint tumbled off the shelf, echoing across the store.

My cheeks went warm, and I quickly picked the cans up before hurrying out into the warm summer evening with Mom right behind me.

She raised her eyebrows. "Are you okay?" she asked.

"Who was that guy with the horse trailer?" I asked. I knew I looked too eager, but I couldn't help it.

Mom sighed. "Oh, honey. Don't get too excited. I did get his number but it's going to take some time."

Not if I get a job and raise the money myself. I bit my lip to keep the words from coming out. Instead I said, "I'm starving. Aren't you?"

She paused for a moment. "Well, what sounds good?"

"Pizza."

⌒⌒⌒

We sat in a booth near the window that had the "Help Wanted" sign. A mixture of garlic and baking bread wafted through the air, causing my stomach to rumble.

A waiter plopped down two menus. "My name's Zane. What can I get you to drink?"

When his bright blue eyes met mine, I stared. Even though the sunlight shone behind him, his eyes seemed luminous, and I couldn't tear my attention away.

"We'll take a couple of waters for now," Mom said.

Zane raised his dark eyebrows and gave me a sparkling smile. Once he left, I picked up the menu and blocked my warming face, hoping to give myself a minute. What just happened? Yes, he was handsome, but I just completely embarrassed myself.

"What sounds good, honey?" she asked.

"You pick," I said and took in a deep breath, trying to get my blushing cheeks under control. *Forget the cute boy for now*. My focus was to get a job.

When Zane came back with our drinks, I couldn't help but notice his eyes again. "Ready to order?" he asked.

"Sure. We'll take a medium supreme, Italian sausage, and garlic on the crust," Mom said and looked at me. "Sound good? Breadsticks or garlic bread?"

"No thanks," I said, thinking that she just saved a few bucks for the fence. After Zane left and Mom got over the surprise of no extras, I decided to spring my surprise. "Did you notice the 'Help Wanted' sign in the window?"

"No, I didn't. Why's that?" Mom said.

"Well, I wondered about getting a job to help out with things."

"Things?"

"Things like the fence and then horses—later. I could walk right over after school and then you could pick me up after work."

"Honey, we just got here. Let's settle in a little before you think about a job," she said and put her face in her hands, rubbing her eyes and around her temples. "I have a lot of things to take care of here in the next few days. Okay."

The "Okay" wasn't said in question form. It was a final statement.

Zane brought our pizza and placed it on the table. I really wanted a horse. Actually, I really wanted Mrs. V to be okay and for Pepe and her to be together again. But realistically, a horse would make me feel a little better, and I really needed a job to get one.

I glanced up at our waiter again as he slid my pizza

onto my plate. He smiled. My cheeks warmed, and I low-ered my head. Out of the corner of my eye, I watched him walk away. Then, when I cut a bite of pizza, another idea formed in the back of my mind.

ℭᴔℭᴔ

I walked toward the back of the restaurant, heading for the sign that said "Restrooms." But when the corner of the wall blocked Mom's view, I stopped at the front counter where Zane stood.

He bent over a piece of paper writing something. He looked up. My throat tightened.

"Ready for the bill?" He handed me the slip of paper. I tried to reach for it but couldn't move just yet.

"Um—" I said in an extremely unsure voice. "I'd like to fill out an application."

His eyebrows went up, and he tilted his chin up in understanding. A manila folder rested behind the cash register.

He reached in and pulled out a piece of paper. "Here you go," he said and handed me a red Pizza Shop pen.

There wasn't much information needed, plus I didn't have much information to give. I'd never had a job, so I filled it out as quickly as I could even though the pen kept slipping in my sweaty hand.

Zane watched. When I stopped at the address line, I looked up. His gaze made me forget what I meant to say.

I looked down at the paper for a moment so I could remember what my question was. "Sorry. I don't know my address yet. We just got here today." I hoped my explanation made sense.

"Oh," he said and leaned a little closer to look at my name. "Well, where did you move to?"

"Outside of town on a dirt road."

"No way! Is it a ranch house in the middle of a corn field?"

I laughed, nervous yet happy to be talking with him. "That's the one."

"Here," he said and reached for the phone book. "The Applegates used to live there."

He found the address and put an old receipt underneath so I could copy the address onto my application. When I finished, I handed it to him.

"You know, we're practically neighbors," he said.

My chest swelled. The thought of Zane being that close made my cheeks warm again. Maybe I could see his house when the corn was gone.

"If I'm working and you need a ride home, I could totally drop you off," he continued.

I smiled, the only thing I could think of to do. "Sure. That would be great." Then I remembered Mom waiting on me. I finished filling out a few more lines and handed it to him. "I'd better get back."

"Sure, no problem," he said and pushed our bill to the edge of the counter like he knew to keep the application a secret. A knowing look passed between us, and I picked up the bill.

"Thanks, Zane," I said.

He smiled, and I felt it, "the connection." My friends had been talking about it last Wednesday before I left. That feeling you get when you meet the perfect guy.

℮ℯℯ

Later that night, I lay in bed, unable to sleep. I rolled over onto my side and faced the wall. Maybe if I shut out all the new shadows, I might be able to fall asleep. My thoughts changed to the start of school in a few short weeks.

We had driven by after we had eaten dinner. The school had two stories, brick with ivy climbing in the shadowed corners, tapering into one at the east side where the sports area started. An awning sheltered the twisting sidewalks so students could walk outdoors from one building to the next if needed. The football field and track looked decent, and the tennis courts weren't too far away.

Mom said they would be starting a soccer team in the next year or two. Maybe I'd try out since I almost made the team last year at my old school, which was three times bigger than this one.

Tamara had made the soccer team. I said I was happy for her, but inside I wasn't quite so sure. She suggested that I be the team manager and help with stuff, that maybe I'd make it next year.

Well, that next year had come, and I was no longer a part of Meridian High School. That thought made me wonder about the name of my new school and what I would be if I made the soccer team. I guessed I'd find out soon enough.

But I wouldn't have time for soccer once I got a horse, which wouldn't be long once I got that job at the Pizza Shop. I rolled over onto my other side and stared at the curtain-less window. Fresh country air floated through the screen, sweet and bitter at the same time, alfalfa and clover. That's what Mom said the farmers baled for horses.

I took a deep breath and tried to relax, knowing I had a lot to do tomorrow, which included painting over this obnoxious pink. Just as my eyelids slowly began to close, the persistent sound of the crickets and the distant bullfrogs suddenly stopped like someone had flipped a switch.

Just like my silent room in the old house.

A numbing panic spread through the fibers of my body, and I felt like I was back at the old house. *This can't be.* I opened my eyes. Not slowly. No. Not me. I opened them fully and completely.

And saw the ghost in the blue dress.

She stood by the window. Her form bright as if she were absorbing the moonlight and amplifying it back into my room. I saw her for only a second or so before she vanished, her eyes leaving behind a red shimmer that looked like hot red coals from a fire pit. I caught only a quick glimpse—enough for me to know she was here.

CHAPTER 11

The next morning, after a sleepless night, I stared at the dark stripe of purple next to the pink when Mom walked in. "How's it coming?"

"I don't like it."

"What do you mean?"

I shook my head and threw the roller into the paint pan, splattering tiny droplets onto the plastic laid out to protect the tan Berber. Mom flinched, eyes searching for any stray drops that may have made it past the barrier.

"It makes me sick," I said. "I need a different color. Something neutral." Something that didn't remind me of my old home. My bare toes crumpled the plastic, and I took a shallow breath. The early morning sun shining through my bedroom windows could not break through the darkness that had settled over me. So I went on. "I don't know why I picked this stupid color again. It's ugly!" Sweat trickled down my temple, and I wiped it away. I took another shallow breath.

"Jenna? Honey? What's gotten into you?"

I could see the surprise in her eyes along with the stress that she'd been under, moving, changing jobs, changing schools.

I wasn't sure if I scared her or worried her, but she turned and left, quietly, taking any and all hope with her. *I just want a different color.* But that wasn't what fueled this emotional turmoil.

Even though a nice breeze sifted through the window, I felt suffocated. My shorts and tank top hung heavy against my skin, sticking to my back and thighs. And my hair, in a high ponytail, felt like it weighed a ton. I wanted to cut it, to release some of the weight and pressure from my head, release the image of those shimmering red eyes.

Now.

I went to the bathroom and rifled through the drawers. No scissors. So I went to the kitchen and searched, realizing that Mom hadn't put much of the kitchen supplies away either. Just when I really needed something.

The box marked "Kitchen" sat over in the corner. I waded through the other boxes, flipped the top open, and found the small shoe box full of knives. Lots of them. These would definitely work. So I picked the biggest one and held it up, the sun glinting off the blade. I wanted to make sure to get through each strand, severing them completely from my head.

"Jenna!" I jumped at the sound of my mother's sharp voice and lost the grip on the knife. It slid down, out of my palm and across my open fingers, slicing the middle and ring finger the deepest. The knife landed in the box of kitchen supplies, causing forks, spoons, and whatever else to clink and rattle. Thin lines of red opened on my fingers, letting the blood run out and down my hand across the life lines of my palm.

"Oh, dear God! What have you done?" Mom zig-zagged through the boxes on her way to me then ripped her shirt off, wrapping it tightly around my fingers and hand. "Get in the truck. We're going to the emergency room."

"It's not that bad, Mom," I said in a calm voice. "It barely got me."

"I *saw* the blood, Jenna. It ran down your hand like you turned a faucet on."

I unwrapped her shirt and made my way to the kitchen sink with her right behind me, almost stumbling over me. With my clean hand I turned on the water and she adjusted it, so it wasn't too hot or cold. Then I put my hand under and watched the blood disappear, swirling down the drain. After it was clean, I pulled it out from under the stream and spread my fingers and palm. The cuts released a little more blood but not much.

"See?" I said. "I told you it wasn't that bad."

She wiped her eyes and then her nose with the shirt and smiled. "Yes. I see," she said and sniffed. "But you still need stitches, especially since it's in the meat of your fingers. That won't heal."

※※※

Mom drove me to the emergency room. The bright sun seemed cheery, like nothing wrong, but I could see the shadows the sun left behind. The shadows were what mattered now. I knew what lurked there.

A nurse stuck my fingers with a needle to numb them, the pain tolerable. Once she left, Mom asked, "So, what were you doing with that knife?" With her elbows on the chair, she placed her hands in a steeple-like position and rested her fingertips against her bottom lip.

I knew this was coming, just not in the emergency room. "I couldn't find the scissors, so I grabbed a knife." She raised her eyebrows at me to continue and gave me a *this-had-better-be-good* look. "At first I wanted to cut the plastic so it laid better but then I decided maybe I should put the lid back on the paint so it didn't dry out before I could get it back to the paint store." I'd had plenty of time on the drive here to come up with this story.

"Keep going."

"I was going to use the heavy handle to tap the lid on and hope we could get back to town soon."

"For what?"

"So the lady could add to the color and make it different." The last part was true, so I hoped it covered up the part that wasn't so true. "She might be able to change it. Then we wouldn't have to buy new paint."

Mom turned her attention to the counter with its computer and gloves and hand sanitizer. I couldn't tell what she was thinking. Normally I could, but with everything that had happened the last few weeks, it felt like we were drifting apart.

Her eyes clouded over and her lips tightened for a moment. It happened so sudden and quick that I wasn't sure it even happened. But when my chest tightened and my pulse quickened, I knew it did, and I knew it wasn't good.

Then the doctor walked in followed by the nurse. "Hello, ladies. I'm Dr. Robbins." He grabbed a pair of gloves and sat on a rolling stool. He rolled it over to my side and took my hand. "Wow. How'd you manage this?" He started working, quickly, quietly. He grabbed a needle shaped like a hook and started closing up the wounds.

"A knife slipped out of my hand." He glanced at me for a moment and then continued fixing my wounds. "It was an accident."

❧❦❧

Once we were done and back on the road, I decided to try my luck. "Are you in a hurry?" Mom looked at me out of the corner of her eye. "I wondered if we could stop by the paint store again."

"I'm tired, honey."

"I'll just take a minute."

"Let's wait and you can bring the paint next time."

"I already brought it. It's in the back."

She narrowed her eyes at me. "I thought it smelled in here." Then instead of turning left to go back home, she veered off and went straight. She turned toward the paint store. I sat a little straighter. She pulled the TrailBlazer next to the front door, and I jumped out, hoping they were open on Sunday.

"I'll see if she can help me first. I'll hurry." I scanned the empty aisles, hurrying from one end to the other, inhaling the old-store smell. The hardwood floor creaked with each step. Finally, the same sales lady appeared.

"Can I help you?"

I raced over to her. "I was just in here yesterday and got some paint and I wondered if you could change the color for me?" I said, rambling along quickly.

"Well, I guess I could turn it brown, if that's what you want," she said, too slow for my taste. *Come on lady, hurry up.* "But you seemed so happy yesterday. What's wrong with it?" she asked, cocking her head to the side.

"Great!" I said, ignoring her question. *She doesn't really care anyway.* I rushed toward the door. "I'll be right back," I said over my shoulder.

Once outside again, I rushed to the open passenger window. "Pop the trunk!"

I hurried to the back. When the hatch clicked open, I grabbed the handle and pulled, exposing all three gallons of paint that I had loaded earlier. Except they weren't as I had left them.

They were tipped over, lids off. Purple paint ran everywhere.

I took a step back. How could this happen? I'd put the lids on tight. There's no way they should've been able to come off. And then I remembered last night and a sick feeling rose in my stomach. Did the ghost do this? And if she did, why? I watched the paint run in a steady stream off the newspaper and onto the carpet.

CHAPTER 12

Later that evening the country air smelled like hay and paint. With the hand-held carpet shampooer, I made another pass over the carpet. I emptied the water for the third time and tackled another pass. *I know I put the lids on tight.* I pulled up more purple paint. The newspaper did catch a lot of it, but it definitely ruined the carpet, according to Mom, anyway. She said she would have to buy some scrap carpet to put down over it. She ordered me to clean as much as possible, so the smell didn't give us a headache every time we went somewhere.

The sun had just begun its evening decent when I decided to call it done. The carpet still had a light tint to it. And, the worse part of all, I was stuck with the same color I had as a child, with one stripe of dark purple. Until I made some money of my own, my walls would remind me of the old house and its memories.

While I rinsed the containers with the water hose, a car rumbled down the road. I dumped the water and rinsed again when the car pulled in the driveway. I glanced up. Zane. My heart fluttered. He switched off the engine and stepped out, bringing with him the faint smell of garlic. Red sauce stained his shirt. I felt my cheeks flush again, but I hoped he attributed it to my hard work.

He eyed the trunk. "What happened here?"

"It's a long story." I stood and wiped the sweat and water from my forehead with the back of my wrist. "A really long story."

He raised his eyebrows and shoved his hands in the pocket of his faded jeans. "If you say so." Once he knew I wasn't going to fill him in, he continued. "I stopped by to let you know that my boss, Saundra, is going to call you tomorrow about a job. She has a few questions about transportation, but I told her you have it covered."

My heart jumped, and I almost dropped the water hose. Not only could I buy my horse but I could also buy some new paint, too. "Really? When do I start?"

He laughed. "Well, you have to have an interview first before she offers you a job."

"When is that?"

"She's calling tomorrow to set it up. Then she'll make up her mind about you. Just a hint—she hates drama."

"What?"

"Drama. You know. Talking about people behind their back, calling in for stupid reasons, causing trouble. Stuff like that."

I looked at the purple carpet then back to Zane. This might not work out after all. The last few days have been nothing but trouble.

"Anyway, here's my number. I work evenings but when school starts, it's mostly weekends."

I reached out and took the torn piece of paper. "Thanks, Zane," I said and smiled.

"No problem," he said and walked to his car, hesitating for a split second before he opened the door. He looked back over his shoulder. "I'll see ya around."

He paused for a moment like he had more to say. But nothing was said. He just climbed in, started the engine, and took off.

The phone number in my hand felt strange. Was he just a friend helping out another friend? Or was he more than that? I turned my attention from the empty driveway back to the stained carpet, then back again. He was so cute. I couldn't wait to ride home with him after work.

After work.

I sucked in a breath. A job! I've got to tell Mom.

I rushed into the house, slamming the front door and forgetting to take off my sandals. "Mom!" I checked the kitchen. She wasn't there. Then I checked the bathroom and living room. I had to tell her the news, but she wasn't there either. I skipped down the hall and checked her bed-room door. Closed. I opened it and peeked in.

There she lay, on her side sleeping, wadded up tis-sues strewn about the bed. Her face looked red and her eyes puffy from crying. My stomach tightened, and I glanced down at my feet. Was she crying because of me?

After I backed out and closed the door, I swallowed hard but the tears still came. I hated to see her upset, es-pecially when it was my fault. I didn't mean to cut my hand or stain the carpet. Determined to work on that stu-pid stain until it was gone, I walked back down the hall, phone number in one hand, stitches in the other.

☾☽☾☽

The next day, I sat on the floor in my bedroom, pull-ing my clothes out of boxes and sorting them. Good school clothes in one pile to put on hangers. Lazy clothes in the other to go in the dresser. Mom and I had already put all my furniture back and cleaned up the plastic from yesterday.

I decided to leave all my wall decorations and Pre-cious Moments, including the one I took from Mrs. V's house, in their boxes until I had finished painting, saving a lot of extra work for me later.

The thin lace-type curtains moved with the wind blowing through the screen. They rushed forward and up only to dance gracefully as they lowered back to their starting point. The wind chimes clinked steadily, recently hung in the tree out back by the deck. Even though my opinion was that wind chimes were creepy, I didn't argue against these because they were a gift to Mom from Mrs. V.

Then I pulled a burgundy tee-shirt from the box and placed it in the pile to go up on hangers. Mom had called to check on Mrs. V again, but she still hadn't improved. Even if we visited her, she wouldn't know we were there.

The room darkened. I could see the gray clouds through my window, angry and gloomy. I debated whether or not to turn the lights on but decided against it. The darkness matched my mood. Saundra from the Pizza Shop hadn't called yet, and it was almost three o'clock in the afternoon. What was she waiting for?

I finished emptying one box and grabbed another, sitting cross-legged as I worked. School sign up began at the end of next week with the first day being the following Tuesday. Mom mentioned school shopping for new shoes and underwear, important stuff, but I declined. I really didn't need anything, just supplies for class. She seemed a bit relieved. I was hoping that would be her reaction when I sprang the new job on her soon.

When I neared the middle of the box, the tempo of the wind chimes picked up. The increasing wind blew through the screen with a soft whistle, causing the curtains to dance with less grace.

The earthy smell of rain filled the room but now

large droplets landed on the windows. I took in a deep breath. Everything smelled better here, even the rain.

I reached farther down into the box, getting close to the bottom, when I noticed the negative change in the air, just like when the ghost in the blue dress appeared. I sat a little straighter and glanced around my room, focusing on the dark corners. No glowing eyes. I looked at the window. She wasn't there either. Fear surged through my veins, leaving my limbs tingling with numbness. I waited. Watched.

But nothing happened.

Finally, I gave up and reached into the box, trying my best to continue unpacking. But when I pulled out the next piece of clothing, fear surged again. I focused. My heart raced, stumbled, got back up, and raced some more. Because there in front of me was my little blue dress.

CHAPTER 13

I wanted to drop the blue dress, but couldn't. It was too beautiful. Horrified, I held the dress with white lace up by the shoulders. Though it had been mine, I didn't feel right touching it. Even in the dim light of my room, the blue was so bright it looked as if it were glowing. My fingertips heated up, warmer, warmer, warmer. But as I started to put it down, my bedroom door burst open. "Jenna! Phone," my mother said strolling in. She laughed when she glimpsed the dress. "Where in heaven did you find this? I thought I'd lost it!"

She pulled it out of my hands and shoved her cell phone in my face. She held the dress by the shoulders, admiring the ruffles and lace. I put the phone to my ear.

"This is Saundra, the manager at the Pizza Shop. I'm calling about an interview."

I didn't say anything. My vocal cords wouldn't work.

"How does tomorrow evening around four o'clock sound?"

I still couldn't speak.

"I can't believe you still have this darling little thing," Mom said and crushed it to her chest. I couldn't help that my attention was on Mom and the dress. "I'm going to put this away for when you get married and have children. How does that sound?" Then she turned and walked out the door.

"Hello?" I heard a voice on the other end. I watched the blue dress disappear. "Jenna? Are you there?"

I cleared my throat. "Sure," I said, trying to regain my senses. "Yes. Tomorrow would be perfect. Thank you for calling." I'd heard my mother say that a million times. I hoped it sounded cool, calm, collected. Somehow I didn't think I came across that way.

After I put the phone down, I flopped back on the floor and threw my hands over my face. *This can't be!* But why my little blue dress? "No, no, no," I said in a low moaning voice.

I pictured the spirit and her evil, menacing look that I'd seen at the old house. The burnt picture frame that I'd left behind the garage. I rolled onto my side and pulled my knees to my chest.

After the numbing feeling started to fade, I stood and found the box marked *FRAGILE!* and opened it. I gently unwrapped Roscoe and my pink blanket, placing them both under the yellow comforter. Then I crawled in and put on my sleep mask.

☙☞☙

The next day, I rode to town for my interview. Mom actually helped me pick out my interview attire. "You should wear navy blue for the best impression. That color means business plus it looks marvelous on you."

I groaned. "But, Mom. It's pizza."

"Doesn't matter. Trust me," she said.

She had twisted my hair into a professional looking bun. I looked like I was being interviewed by a bank.

When we got into town, the stop lights glowed brighter against the overcast sky. Yesterday's rain storm left an eerie aftermath, which was supposed to last another couple of days, but the sun kept trying to burn through, anyway. We pulled in front of the Pizza Shop and parked.

Mom checked the clock on the truck. "It's almost time. You're a little early, but I'd go in anyway and wait for her. I'll get some grocery shopping done and be back soon."

I leaned over and hugged her. "Thanks, Mom."

"Good luck, honey," she said and kissed my cheek.

I walked into the Pizza Shop and up to the counter. Zane walked over, wiping his hands on a towel. He had a small spot of flour on his cheek, and I had a sudden and overwhelming desire to wipe it off. "Where've you been? You're late!"

"What? I'm early!"

"She expected you at four o'clock." I felt the blood drain from my face. This wasn't good.

A second later, a lady appeared around the corner. "Jenna?" Her black hair color looked drastic against her fair complexion.

"Yes," I said and swallowed, forcing my recently eaten strawberry yogurt back down to my stomach.

"You're late. Follow me," she said and turned. I followed her down the short hall and glanced back at Zane before entering her office.

He shrugged his shoulders. A stack of papers on one side of her desk balanced the computer screen on the other. Small, just like the kitchen we had passed. And warm from the oven that sat on the other side of the wall. She closed the door behind me.

"I'm sorry. I thought you said five o'clock over the phone," I said.

"You sounded distracted, so I even wondered if you'd show up. Anyway, tell me about yourself," she said and took a seat behind the old wooden desk. Her chair squeaked.

I paused. Tell her about myself? Where do I begin? *I'm fifteen and I can't seem to have a normal life? That trouble follows me everywhere?* "I really like pizza," I said instead and smiled.

She chuckled and wrote something on my application. "Why do you want to work here?"

Mom quizzed me on the way here about these interview questions, but my mind couldn't recall anything at the moment. "I would like to earn some money for a horse fence and to help out at home."

Saundra raised her eyebrows. "Not because we're a good place of employment or this would be a rewarding and challenging job?"

"That, too. Yes," I said and mentally smacked myself on the forehead. She scribbled again on my application. I leaned forward a little, trying to make out her writing when she asked another question.

"What about transportation?"

I leaned back. "I have it covered. Plus, I'll be sixteen in a month."

She raised her eyebrows at this. "Yes. I see," she said and put down her pen. She sat back in her chair, resting her hands over her large midsection. "Tell me, are you going to be okay working Friday and Saturday nights when your friends are out having fun?"

I paused for a bit, obviously taken off guard. "I guess so. I mean—I'm new here, so I don't really have any friends, and I really need the money."

She nodded and continued. "I will be interviewing the rest of this week and then make my decision. Do you have any questions or is there anything else you would like to say about yourself?"

My mind still couldn't recall anything Mom had said earlier. Couldn't remember what I should say at this point. "Not really."

She stood and walked over to her office door. She opened it. "It was nice meeting you, Jenna." She ushered me out then closed the door. I turned around and stared at the lost opportunity. Everything that had seemed to fall into place just fell apart in the matter of a five-minute interview.

"Everything go okay?" Zane asked. The small spot of flour was still on his face, but the desire to wipe it off now gone.

"Not really," I said and walked down the hall and out the front door.

I knew if I didn't get out of there soon, Zane would witness a breakdown. I walked across the street, not really paying attention to the traffic. A car honked its horn, but I didn't care. Once I walked into the paint store, I made my way to the restroom in the back.

I closed the door and locked it. Leaning my forehead against the back of the door, I let the tears tumble down my cheeks. *I can't do this.* I took in a deep breath. *I can't do this alone.* I'd barely made it through the last couple of months. Moving should have fixed things, but instead it has made things worse. Out of control.

I sucked in a shaky breath. When I finally calmed down, I wiped my face with some tissue paper and blew my nose. The complexion that stared back at me from the mirror was still sallow, and the dark under eye circles looked worse. I needed to do something. Something that would destroy the ghost—before she destroyed me.

ↄﾟ⌒ↄﾟ⌒

An hour later, Mom and I drove home in silence. She asked about the interview. I said it went okay, but I couldn't look at her. I didn't want her to see my puffy eyes. The evening was winding down as we drove past one field after another. Soybeans, then corn. Once in a while a hayfield. We pulled into the driveway and parked, but she didn't turn off the engine.

"It's all right, honey. You'll find yourself a job when the time is right."

I didn't answer.

"I didn't like the idea at first, but I know you are just trying to help out." She glanced over at me, but I sat still, staring at the dashboard. "This will give you time to get situated in school. Maybe try out for some sports or join a club or something."

I sighed and looked out the window, so she couldn't see my watering eyes.

"I still think you're a little young for a job anyway. It takes a lot of responsibility to work for someone and perform a task up to their standards. Be there on time when you're scheduled." She paused for a second. I knew she wanted me to understand, or at least say I did.

I folded my arms across my chest.

"I also wanted to tell you that I'm starting my job early. They had an employee leave unexpectedly, so they're moving my start date up," she said.

I shifted in my seat. "But I don't want you to start early. I don't want to be here alone."

"School starts next week, honey. It's not long."

"Please?"

She sighed. "I don't really have a choice. They want me to start tomorrow."

I leaned my head back.

"If you need something, call Grandma and Grandpa. They'll be here Saturday for a visit. Give us a chance to settle in."

I sat there, taking in the information, my silence the only thing needed to show my disagreement. She sighed and shook her head. Then she turned off the engine and stepped out of the truck, leaving me in the evening heat.

If only I could tell her that I needed her right now. That a ghost had been haunting me since Dad died. And I wasn't sure what to do.

Then maybe she wouldn't leave me here alone, knowing that I was afraid.

CHAPTER 14

That night, the sky darkened with a slight glow on the horizon, like the sun had finally beaten the clouds and didn't want to give up on the day. Mom had already gone to bed, but I wasn't tired. It'd been two nights since I'd seen the ghost in the blue dress here at the new house. And now, I just wanted out, to get some fresh air.

I grabbed a flashlight and headed outside to the barn. A weak beam illuminated the way. When I got there, I opened the side door and stepped in.

The barn had two sliding doors, a large one for hay and a small one for the horse to come in and out of the pasture. Cracks covered the cement floor with tall weeds growing in all directions. It wasn't the best, but I would make it work. I moved along through the barn, bending over and pulling the weeds, mentally fixing up the place. Over in the corner, near the small door, I imagined a tall horse, maybe a palomino.

While I stared at the corner, a noise at the door caught my attention. My body stiffened. I stood frozen, searching for the negativity I always felt with the ghost. Nothing. But the feeling that someone was watching became overwhelming, and I couldn't move. Footsteps behind me.

"Jenna?"

I jumped, screamed, and dropped the flashlight all at the same time. It landed with a loud crack and the light went out. Darkness.

"Jenna? It's me, Zane!"

It took a moment for his voice to break through the fear. But once it did, I turned around. He had retreated to the barn door. The faint light from the moon outlined his silhouette.

Even though I should've been too scared, I noticed the width of his shoulders, broad and strong. "I was coming home from work and saw a light in your barn. Thought I'd check it out," he said. He stuck his hands in his pocket and shrugged his shoulders. "If it was a burglar, then I would have caught him. But I'm glad it was you instead."

I swallowed, not sure what to say, only glad he was here. Now I wasn't alone. I walked over to him. He smelled like fresh cologne with garlic undertones.

"I didn't mean to scare you," he said, his voice low, almost a whisper. He leaned toward the door, uncertain. "Maybe I should go."

I took a breath in. "No. Don't go." I reached out and touched his forearm. My fingertips rested only for a second before falling to my side, but it was enough. He shifted his weight, and I knew that second had convinced him to stay. "I'm glad you came by. I don't want some burglar steeling all the weeds." We both let out a nervous laugh. "Want to sit on the deck with me?" I asked, hopeful.

"Actually, I was wondering if you wanted to go swimming."

"Really? Isn't it kinda late? Where would we even go?"

"There's a small lake just down the road here."

I hesitated, wondering if I should wake Mom up or just stay home. Then I looked at Zane again and wanted to go with him. I'd go anywhere as long as it was away from here.

"I'll grab my suit," I said then turned and ran back inside, my heart pounding, only this time in a good way.

೧೯೧೩

We drove down my dirt road in the opposite direction, a direction that I'd never been. Cornfields surrounded us until we came to a stop sign. He turned left and

drove around a few curves until the headlights illuminated a small dirt trail. Tall trees lined the trail as we drove
deep into the woods. If we'd met another car, one of us
would have had to turn around.

The moonlight reflected off of the surface of the water, and I straightened to get a better look. Zane parked
off to the side. It was a small lake surrounded by trees
except for the small beach. A fishing pier reached out
from the shore off to the right.

"Follow me," Zane said, leading the way. "I bet the
water's a little cold from the rain, but it'll still be fun."

He shot me a grin and my stomach did butterfly flip
flops. So, I followed. I sat to his right at the end of the
pier, my towel beneath me.

"So," he said. "Where did you move from?"

"Indianapolis."

"Big city girl? Why move here, then?"

"My dad passed away back in June from cancer. Co-
lon cancer. And my mom wanted to live closer to her
parents and this is where we ended up." I looked down at
the waves that our feet were making as we moved them
back and forth.

He cleared his throat and looked out across the small
pond. "I'm sorry to hear about your dad."

"Thanks," I said. I didn't want to talk about Dad anymore. It still hurt, so I moved on. "Things are kinda
tough right now, so I believed I'd help out by getting a
job. Then I go and blow it."

Zane let out a small laugh. "Saundra wasn't impressed—"

I flinched at his words. Knowing I blew it was one thing, but hearing Zane say the words was another.

"But don't worry," Zane said quickly when he noticed my frustration. "I'll put in a good word for you."

A feeling of despair swirled inside me. I concentrated on the water, swallowing my emotions. I had to get my mind on something else, or I was going to cry. "What about you?" I asked and hoped he didn't notice the thickness of my voice.

He shrugged. "Not much to say about me except that I'm on the basketball team. I'm the point guard. My junior year, we lost sectionals because another guy didn't catch my pass. Totally his fault." He looked at me.

I nodded as if I were listening. But instead, I watched a massive line of clouds that had gathered on the other side of the small lake. It seemed like they were hovering, waiting.

"I'm hoping we win this time. That'd be the best way to end my senior year." With his excitement, he kicked his feet in the water and his arm and shoulder brushed mine. Water splashed up on my legs. I tore my attention away from the clouds and focused on him. How did he get so close?

"Now back to you," he said. "Any big plans when you get out of high school?"

I looked out over the water and thought about my future. And about how close he sat. I could feel the warmth of his skin and the softness of the hair on his arms. His closeness made me feel normal for a moment.

But the feeling faded when the moon slid behind a massive line of dark clouds. I noticed that the clouds were no longer hovering but moving in our direction. A distinct line of darkness started on the other side of the lake and moved toward us like a wall. And with it came an uneasy feeling. The closer it got, the more uneasy I felt.

Then the uneasiness turned to the heaviness I had felt by the stairway in the old house, and I knew. I knew she was near. Even though I hadn't seen her yet, I could feel her.

He moved closer, and so did the clouds.

Zane cleared his throat. "Any boyfriends back home?"

I couldn't answer. The wall was coming. "I think we should go," I said and stood. Once on my feet, I reached down, grabbed Zane by his upper arm, and pulled. Shocked, he rose to his feet. Once he stood, I turned and ran the length of the pier to the beach. "Hurry," I called over my shoulder.

"What'd I say?" Zane asked, not far behind me. "What's going on?"

The sand seemed as if it were grabbing my feet with each step I took. I turned and chanced a look at the sky, to see the clouds, but I stumbled on something, maybe a rock, I wasn't sure. I lost my balance and fell to my hands and knees. My chest tightened. A sharp pain shot through my hand. Zane came up behind me and helped me to my feet. With his arm draped around my waist, we continued to the car together.

As if he knew something was wrong, Zane started the car, backed up, and took off. On the way home, he glanced at me more than a few times, but he stayed silent. I fluffed my towel over the hand that hurt, not wanting to say anything about the fish hook embedded in the palm of my hand. Enough had happened tonight, and I was already afraid that I'd scared him off.

When he pulled his Mustang into the drive, he turned. "Listen," he said, "I'm not sure what happen—"

"I'm sorry." I searched for an excuse, something believable. "It was just that I started to not feel good, and I didn't want to get sick in front of you. I hope I'm not coming down with something." I took in a deep breath and looked at him.

A small indentation between his eyebrows signaled his concern and confusion. It looked like he wanted to say more. So did I. I wanted to confide in him, but I didn't.

I couldn't. And I wouldn't.

I wouldn't do that to him, knowing that the ghost in the blue dress had somehow followed me. How? I didn't know.

I got out of the car and kept my hand to my side.

He leaned over and looked at me through the passenger side window. "I guess I'll see ya around?" The pitch of the last word came out as a question instead of a statement.

"Okay," I said, not sure what else to say. When I stepped away from the car, he hesitated for a moment before he left. There was nothing more I could say or do except watch the car's glowing red taillights in the dark until they were gone.

☙❧❧

I sat on the edge of my bed, rocking gently back and forth, holding my hand. The darkness of my room hid everything except my fear and the pain in my palm. For the moment, I needed to push that fear away, so I took a deep breath and walked into the bathroom. The sharp point of an old rusted fishhook was sunk into my palm, close to the thumb area.

I pulled out a bottle of peroxide and poured it over the wound, causing it to bubble.

Okay, so I disinfected it. Now what? I sucked in a breath, grabbed the end of the hook, and pulled. But not for long. The pain was too much. I flexed my hand for a better look. The entire end was embedded. There was only one other option.

"What do you mean you fell?" Mom turned on the lamp and blinked, trying to focus on me. Zane and I had sat on the pier longer than I expected, because when I looked at her clock it read almost midnight.

"I fell in the barn."

"What were you doing in the barn?"

"I couldn't sleep."

"Well, are you okay?" she asked and yawned.

"No," I said and sat down on the bed next to her.

Then I showed her my hand. I had already tried to get the hook out on my own, which caused it to bleed and hurt even worse. The fact that I deserved it made it easier to bear the pain. Not only had I lied to her, but I was about to ruin her first day of work. The emergency room was the only solution.

The same emergency room doctor, Dr. Robbins, who'd stitched my other hand, removed the fish hook. "Did you miss me?" he asked when he walked into the room.

I tried to smile, no big deal, but the smile wasn't genuine. And he could tell. Once he numbed my hand, it didn't take long.

"Thanks," I said.

He put the last bandage on my hand and pressed it firmly into place. "I hope I don't see you again anytime soon," Dr. Robbins said and stood.

With that, I actually smiled. He squeezed my shoulder and left. The nurse handed Mom the discharge papers.

During the quiet ride home, my conscience almost

got the best of me a few times. I wanted to tell her the truth, but I didn't. I knew she would be crushed that I had left the house without telling her. And even more crushed that I had lied to her this whole time. So I stayed quiet. I stayed quiet, because I didn't want to hurt her.

CHAPTER 15

The next day, another fear entered my mind as I showered and washed my hair, being careful of my new wound. What if I had to tell Mom about the ghost? Would she believe me? I didn't have any proof. No ghostly writings on the wall or objects flying around on their own. Plus Mrs. V was still in the nursing home, so she wouldn't be able to help.

I wouldn't want her to help, either. The guilt had been unbearable. If she died, I wouldn't be able to go on with a normal life. Normal. I wished things were normal again. To go back in time when Dad was still here. No ghosts crawling out of pictures.

My palm throbbed when I reached down to turn off the water. The doctor said most of the damage came from me wrenching on it to avoid the trip to the emergency room. But if I had gotten it out, I wouldn't have had to lie to Mom.

I stepped out and dried off, tying my hair up in the towel to soak up the excess water. After I threw on my robe, I walked into my room and over to my closet, gently running my fingers from one hanger to the next, looking, thinking.

I wandered over to my bed and flopped down. With my hands above my head, I stared at the ceiling, breathing in the smell of fresh-cut grass blowing in my window. Most of the chores were marked off the list Mom left this morning, except for a few. Things I could do later. Things that really didn't matter. She was just trying to keep me busy all day. Fine by me.

My tired eyes ached, and I closed them. *Just for a bit*, I told myself. My breathing became rhythmic and the sound of chirping birds faded into my dream...

ᕮᕤᕮᕤ

Laughter bounced off the walls of the old house back in Indianapolis. I ran up the stairway. I was a child again.

"Be careful, honey," my dad said. "Don't fall down the steps. I may not be here to catch you."

When I reached the top of the stairway, I instinctively turned left and ran along the balcony. At the end of the hallway, a closed door.

I reached out and my four-year-old fingers turned the

doorknob and pushed the door open. I stepped inside the room.

In the corner was a ghostly outline of a small bed with what looked like a child underneath the quilted blankets, her hair long lying gently behind her in curls on the bedspread. She stirred, and I thought I heard a muffled cough. But I wasn't sure.

"Sissy?" she asked.

She tried to turn over. But before I could see her face, Mom walked in.

"What do you think?" she said, and I jumped. The ghostly apparition disappeared. Mom laughed and then gave me a big kiss. "This must be your new room."

She opened her arms and spun once through the middle. Then she dropped her arms and sighed. While I watched, her expression lit up, and I knew Dad had just walked in.

"We could paint it a different color for you, honey," he said and leaned against the door jam with his arms crossed.

"No. Pink's my fav-oo-rite," I said and nodded once, firmly.

✪✪✪

The dream faded, and the chirping birds returned. My eyes ached when I opened them. I leaned up on my elbow and checked the time. Five o'clock.

I had a strange sense of lost time, followed by confusion. My dream had seemed so real, like I was really there. Having been just a kid, I didn't remember our first day at the house. Unsteady, I stood and held onto my bedpost. When my head cleared, I walked to my closet.

Midway across the room, I felt something strange. I felt the presence of the ghost. I stopped, frozen in the middle of my room. The hair on my arms and neck prickled even though a warm evening breeze blew through the window. I turned around. She lay on my bed with her back to me, only her blonde wavy curls visible, covered with the same quilts from my dream.

"Sissy?"

I took a step back, but that wasn't enough. The desire to distance myself from the ghost grew and I took another step, step, step backward until I was pressed against the wall. I could feel the ghost's need for her sister. It pulled at my very center, twisting, molding until I felt the same way. It felt so real that I couldn't move. I stood by the wall and stared until the apparition disappeared.

❧❧❧

Later in the week, on a Thursday afternoon, I worked on my list of chores. I had seen the ghost twice now, and I didn't know what to do about it. Seeing her in my bed after such a strange dream scared me. And the feelings of missing a sister that I didn't have also scared me. What did she want? She must want something to follow me this far.

Just as I finished wiping the counters in the kitchen, I felt her presence. The negativity in the air increased and my heart rate shot up along with the hairs on the back of my neck. With washcloth in hand, I searched for her.

She stood at the end of the hall, right outside my mother's room. The form, a little blurrier than normal and not as brilliant, faced Mom's bedroom door like she was looking through it. She took a step forward and reached out her hand to turn the doorknob. But before she even touched it, she walked right through the door.

The negativity in the air disappeared, and my heart rate returned to almost normal. I walked to the end of the hall and stopped. *What was she doing?* I looked at the closed door and considered the only reason I wanted to enter Mom's room. The blue dress, tucked away somewhere, being saved for something special.

Was that what the ghost was looking for? Every time she appeared, she was wearing it. Could the dress be the link? But that wouldn't make any sense, because the dress was mine.

For some reason, though, I didn't like the dress being in the house, but I didn't know what to do next. So I turned the doorknob and stepped into Mom's room. The headboard of the bed sat up against the wall to my right with the dresser to the left, the window straight ahead, with her cedar chest sitting below it.

I made my way through her room and knelt down in front of the chest, I ran my fingers over the shiny wood. A few nicks and scratches decorated the bottom of it but the top was flawless. A knitted afghan with burgundy and blue lay folded off to the side, one that her great grandma had made for her. I carefully picked it up and placed it on the floor.

The filtered sun came through the sage green curtains, giving the room a softness fitting for Mom. A twinge of guilt crept through me. For one thing, I was snooping, and, second, she loved that little dress. I pictured her crushing it to her chest like a long lost teddy bear.

Not sure of my plan, whether I would burn the dress or not, I reached for the lid of the cedar chest. I just wanted to see it. I still had a few days to make up my mind. School didn't start until next week. I just wanted to touch it, then maybe I would miraculously know what to do. But when I pulled on the lid, it didn't move. Even with two hands, it didn't budge. I bent to inspect why it wouldn't open.

Locked.

ɛ৲ɔɛ৲ɔ

I stared at the cedar chest for a moment and wondered why Mom would lock it. The more I dwelled on it, the more curious I got. A knock sounded at the door. I jumped up. My pulse took off down the hall, and I followed.

Halfway to the front door, I remembered the afghan. Not knowing who was here, I knew had better leave things the way they were. So I turned and raced back to her room, placing the blanket back on top of the cedar chest. Nothing else had been moved. I shut the door and took a deep breath to calm myself. I would unlock the cedar chest later.

I walked to the front door and opened it. Zane stood wearing a pair of swimming trunks and flip flops. My stomach fluttered.

"What took you so long?" he asked.

I couldn't believe it. I was sure he wouldn't want to talk with me again after the way I acted the other night. I guess he didn't think I was a freak after all. I fought the urge to jump up and down.

"I was just cleaning," I said, trying to control the excitement in my voice. "What're you doing?"

He looked down at his swim trunks and shrugged. "Swimming. Wanna come?"

With some things still on my to-do list and fresh guilt from recently lying to Mom, I hesitated for a moment. But would I be lying now? She was still at work. She'd never have to know.

"How long would we be gone?" I asked.

He shrugged. "Not long."

I paused, just for a second. Chores or Zane? I was

tired of being alone. I wanted friends. Being with Zane won. "Sounds good. Let me change." In my bedroom, I found my turquoise polka dotted bikini in the bottom of the closet, not as pretty as the burgundy one I wore before, but I put it on anyway. Didn't want to wear the same one again.

I put on a pair of shorts and a shirt then slipped my bare feet into my sandals. After I grabbed a towel and sunglasses, I shut the front door without locking it since I didn't have a spare key yet.

When I hopped in, a girl and another guy sat in the backseat.

"Hi. I'm Samantha," the girl said. Her voice bubbled to the front of the car. Zane backed out of the driveway and started for the lake. "So, what are you this year?"

"Sophomore," Zane said and turned to check with me. "Right?"

I nodded.

"We're all seniors," Samantha said, her voice high and soft. "I'm a cheerleader and Trey and Zane play basketball."

"I did try out for soccer," I said. "But I didn't make the team last year."

Sam leaned forward all excited. "We're finally starting soccer this year. You should try out!"

"Sure!" I couldn't help my enthusiasm. I was so excited to be out of the house and with new friends.

We drove back the same long drive as before and

parked off to the left again. Zane came around the car and stood next to me while Trey and Sam got out. Then Zane reached around me, his arm slightly brushing my shoulder, and pushed the car door shut. My heart flip flopped along with my sandals, and we followed Trey and Sam to the pier. The sun beat down on us as we walked to the end.

Sam and Trey stopped. "What the hell happened here?" Trey said and bent down, inspecting the pier.

We all crowded around. I peeked over Samantha's shoulder to see. The wood of the pier appeared blackened and splintered upward where lightning had struck— exactly where Zane and I had been sitting the other night.

An uneasy feeling churned within my stomach, and I quickly sat before my legs had the chance to crumble.

"Are you okay?" Zane's voice echoed as if he was talking into a tin can.

He put his hand on my shoulder. Any other time, the touch of his hand would have sent pleasurable shivers through my body.

But not this time.

He took a step back and peered down at me. So did Trey and Samantha.

"You look pale." Samantha studied my face. "You're not gonna to puke, are ya?"

All three stared at me, but I couldn't answer. They didn't know. How could they? How could they know that the lightning strike wasn't really caused by lightning?

That it was a warning. That the ghost was changing, be-coming unpredictable. How could they know that, if they didn't stay away from me, they would all be in danger?

CHAPTER 16

Where *have* you been? I've been worried sick!" Mom said and stomped from the kitchen.

I closed the living room door. The noise of Zane's car pulling out of the driveway caught her attention. She rushed to the window and looked to see who I'd been with.

"No note," she continued, turning her attention back to me. "Nothing!" She went back into the kitchen, grabbed a Kleenex, and dabbed her eyes. Her lip started to tremble and her anger turned to something else.

"We just lost track of time," I said, still standing just inside the door with my towel in my arms. I'd hurt her again. "I went to the lake with some friends. That's all." Even though I really didn't go swimming, I couldn't with my stitches. I'd wanted to come home, but I didn't want to ruin their fun. So I just sat on the pier, twisting my towel, waiting until Zane was ready to leave. Why couldn't Mom understand that asking my new friends to leave early would've been social suicide? She lowered her head and brought the Kleenex up to her eyes. "It's no big deal, Mom." My voice soft.

She took a deep breath and composed herself. "What am I going to do with you?" she asked and then whipped her hard stare toward me. Her shoulder length hair swung gracefully with the movement. "Temper tantrums, anger issues, and now you just leave when you want to." Her voice rose another level. "You're going to start seeing a therapist." She pointed her finger at me.

I flinched. Not because of her finger pointing, but because she thought I needed professional help. Only troubled people got counseling.

She tore her stare away and focused on the kitchen wall. Her chest heaved. She wiped her cheeks again with the Kleenex.

The pain of hurting her slowly started to morph into something else—exhaustion. I was tired. Tired of being afraid. Tired of feeling guilty about Mrs. V. Tired of missing Pepe. And most of all, tired of not having any friends. I just wanted an evening with some new friends.

I sighed. "Mom, you have no idea what I'm going through," I said in a slow, low voice. "I just needed some time to myself."

She continued to stare at the kitchen wall, but her chest heaved less. Maybe she was calming down.

"I should've left a note. I'm sorry."

"You're grounded," she said, her tone flat, unemotional, as if she didn't care about my side of the story.

My jaw tightened. I could feel a storm of emotions roiling inside of me. How could she be so unfair? Didn't she care about me anymore? I threw my towel on the floor and stomped to my room. I lay on my bed, too upset to cry. I wanted to get up and throw things. My lamp, my alarm clock, even my computer. But I didn't. I was too tired.

❧❧❧

After my shower that night, I applied the prescription cream to the cut on my hand. The stitches didn't need anything. They were healing just fine. No sign of Mom. I sighed and allowed the hollow feeling to consume me. What was I thinking? Running off with no note. No phone call to let her know where I was. *I will never do that again*, I promised.

I shut my bedroom door, turned off the lights, and flopped down on my bed. I let my mind wander. My thoughts turned to my dream about the first day in the old house and the little girl sleeping in the bed. Was it the ghost? It had to be. I sifted through the details, trying to find some clue as to who she was and maybe how to de-

stroy her. She hasn't hurt me yet, but she hurt Mrs. V and
could easily hurt someone else with the lightning strike at
the pier proof enough.

I rolled over and pulled my pink blanket up under
my chin. The curtains danced in the breeze. What had the
ghost been doing outside Mom's room? The chimes tinkled here and there in the soft night wind. Distant crickets
sounded like a country lullaby. My heavy eyelids closed,
and I drifted into a hazy dream...

ᑫᔆᑫᔆ

I was in my old room. Car lights bounced off the
pink walls, causing strange shadows to appear in the corner of the room. With a firm grip on my pink blanket, I
yanked it up and over my eyes. But not for long. A
strange heaviness overtook the air. I lowered my blanket
and looked around my room. In the distant corner sat a
bed with a little girl in it.

She coughed, a weak, painful cough. The quilts
looked old and heavy with the bed frame of simple
wrought iron. She stirred, her back still to me.

A faint voice asked, "Sissy?" A moment later, a
grown woman's silhouette walked out of the wall. I
gasped, and my heart thumped. I just hoped the strange
lady couldn't see me.

Her hair swept up in a bun, she wore a long dress
that came up around her neck with lace. She walked

across the room with determination and sat at the edge of the bed. She placed one hand on the little girl's back and the other on her forehead for a moment. When she finished, she looked up suddenly, as if remembering something important. While I watched, she turned her dark face toward me.

Startled, I pulled my pink blanket over my head, not sure if she had actually seen me. My little heart thumped wildly in my chest, echoing in my ears. The heaviness lifted, slowly. Maybe she had disappeared by now. I didn't hear anything, no cough or whispers from the little girl. When I couldn't stand it any longer, I lowered my blanket.

ↅↄↅↄ

But I woke. The soft sound of crickets and wind chimes drifted into my room. Even though it was only a dream, my entire body shook. To make sure I was awake, I blinked a few times and rolled over, hugging my knees to my chest. Why these strange dreams? Maybe there *was* something wrong with me.

My room seemed exceptionally dark, and I didn't like it. A room full of light sounded better. I threw my blankets back and launched myself off of the bed, landing far enough away that the lady from my dream couldn't snatch my ankles and pull me under into the darkness, a darkness that I wanted to avoid.

When I flipped on the lights, I quickly searched my room. Empty. Even though my bright room housed nothing scary, I still had no relief.

I lay back down, lights still on. Even though the woman's stare in my dream didn't seem evil, it still haunted me, mostly blank with a hint of something I couldn't put my finger on. I pulled Roscoe close and braced for another sleepless night.

ೕ๛ೕ๛

Later the next day, I studied the list of chores Mom had left on the kitchen counter. Mow the yard. Done. Sweep and dust. Done. With my grandparents coming tomorrow, she wanted everything to look perfect, like everything was okay. Under control.

With the list done, I still held off going into Mom's room. It was something that, once I started, I had to finish. The point of no return. Just like in the movies where the main character was about to execute their plan and everything turned out perfectly or went horribly wrong. The end.

Except right now, I wasn't sure. I'd burned the picture, and she followed me. Lately, she'd been invading my dreams, like she was trying to tell me something. Or trying to make me understand. Was the sick girl in the bed her?

But the urge to open the chest was strong, to see the

dress again. When I held it in my hands, for just those few seconds after pulling it out of the box, I had a strange feeling. Something I couldn't describe. I tried not to think about it, but it was still there, on the tip of my fingers, like a word that just wouldn't come to mind when needed.

And since I'd found out Mom had locked the chest, that urge intensified. The urge won. And I ignored my gut feeling to leave everything alone. A feeling that said to not go where I'm not supposed to. I started down the hall to Mom's room.

The door was slightly cracked. I pushed it open and walked in. The cedar chest sat across the room beneath the double bay window. I looked around, searching for the perfect hiding spot for a small key.

There on the dresser sat her jewelry box. Three little drawers lined the left side with a glass door on the right, where her necklaces hung. I opened each drawer and rummaged around. Rings on the bottom, bracelets in the middle one, and what looked like earrings and a few things from her childhood in the top.

Nothing yet.

I opened the right side and admired her diamond pendant necklace that Dad had given her for their anniversary before he died. The light in the room bounced off the beautifully cut edges. I spun the wheel at the top and looked for a hanging key.

Nothing. I moved the jewelry box over just to make

sure she hadn't slid it underneath. Nope. I looked around the room again. There were hundreds of places she could put a tiny key.

I sighed and turned back to the jewelry box. This was the best bet. Where would I hide a key? I paused for a moment before picking it up and looking underneath. My heart gave a quick thud against my chest. She'd taped the key to the bottom.

With my hands shaking, I carefully peeled the key from the bottom of the jewelry box and walked to the chest. I moved the afghan off to the side once again. Once the key was in the lock, I turned it until it made a clicking sound.

I took a deep breath and raised the lid. The chest held item after item, all the way to the top. There were a few old books, lots of photo albums, and what looked like her wedding gown sticking out from the bottom.

A brown leather photo album caught my attention, and I picked it up. Family pictures. I looked at the first one, the most recent before Dad died. We were all still at the old house. I laughed at a picture of me putting an ice cube down his shirt when we were grilling.

I turned the page and saw another picture of Mom and Dad, one that I must've taken when they weren't looking. Mom smiled at Dad, but he stared off, not paying attention. There in person, but his mind elsewhere. My heart ached.

I quickly flipped through the rest of the pictures.

Most of them I had seen already. After I tucked them back into the photo album, another picture in the right upper corner grabbed my attention. Tenderly, I picked it up, looking closely at the smiling images.

My Dad had his arms wrapped around my shoulders with my cheek pressed to his. It seemed like only yesterday when he passed away, leaving a hole in our family, a hole in me. Dad, always the fun one, let me sleep over at friends' houses when Mom said I was too young, and he would take me for ice cream before supper. And he was the one who bought Roscoe for me. My chest ached and the hollow feeling consumed me.

Tears formed in my eyes and then took their time before they ran down my cheeks. I took a couple of deep breaths and ran my finger over the picture. Maybe I'd take it and make a copy for myself, return it before Mom even missed it.

A rumbling sound came down the dirt road. Mom. I grabbed the rest of the pictures, stuffed them into the back of the album, and put it back into the cedar chest. I closed the lid and put the afghan back on top. Everything looked the same as it did before.

Just as Mom's TrailBlazer pulled into the driveway, I noticed an envelope lying on the floor. I picked it up, and hurried to my bathroom. I didn't have time to put it back since it had been left behind.

CHAPTER 17

I sat on the bathroom floor holding the envelope. It was in Dad's handwriting, addressed to me with the word "confidential" under my name. It had been previously sealed, but now it was open. My fingers slid underneath the ragged edge of the envelope lip and pulled out a piece of paper. It read:

My Dear Jenna,
I hope what I write in this letter doesn't mean anything to you, but I have to write it be-fore I'm gone. I have a very uneasy feeling, and the closer I get to passing on, the worse it gets. I'm not sure if what I'm seeing is real or just my imagination with all the medication and such, but I have a feeling I need to warn you. Please

be careful, honey. Remember, always keep me in
your heart. I'll always be there for you.
    Love, Dad

The garage door slammed, and footsteps echoed in
the kitchen. Bags rustled and groceries clunked against
the counter. "Jenna! I'm home!" Mom's footsteps sounded down the other hallway to her bedroom.

I looked at the envelope again. It was supposed to be
for me only! How could she open it? How could she keep
it from me? The bathroom had fogged over, and my eyes
filled, blurring my vision even more. I brought my knees
up and wrapped my arms around them, hoping that this
would comfort me.

My mouth went dry. I swallowed. It felt like there
was something in my throat, thick and unmovable. I
swallowed again and tilted my head back against the
wall, tears sliding down my cheeks. Dad had known.

As a kid, I tried to tell him about the ghost. He patted
my hand and assured me that it was "just my imagination." This letter was to tell me I was right. There was a
ghost, and he was trying to warn me. The proof was in
my trembling hands.

I tucked the envelope into the bottom drawer underneath the tampons and pads. Then I slipped out of my
clothes and into the warm shower, letting the water run
over my face and hair. If I had seen this letter, had a
warning of some sort, Mrs. V would be okay.

തിരുജ

After my shower, I went to my room. But before I climbed into bed, I went to my top dresser drawer and opened it. Carefully I unwrapped Mrs. V's Precious Moments figurine. I held it with both hands, closed my eyes, and thought of Mrs. V. What would she tell me right now that would make me feel better? What would she do?

I imagined her voice in my head, telling me everything was going to be okay. I imagined her caring hand on my back, the smell of her perfume, the smell of Pepe's doggy shampoo, the weight of his little body on my lap.

"Jenna, dinner!" Mom called.

Her high-pitched, sing-song voice startled me and pulled me from my daydream. Gently, I rewrapped the figurine in bubble wrap and placed it in the back of my dresser drawer. I didn't answer Mom right away. I couldn't bring myself to.

After I had climbed into bed, the door opened. "Honey?"

"I don't feel good," I said.

"What's wrong?"

She came and sat next to me. She reached out for my hand, and I pulled away. I couldn't help it. She blinked quickly and looked away. But not before I'd seen the look on her face.

I'd hurt her again. No guilt consumed me this time. I wasn't capable of having any feelings at the moment. She stood and left, closing my door softly behind her. No prodding. No questions.

Even with the warmth of the evening, I had all my blankets pulled up under my chin. I couldn't get warm. The sunlight that filtered into my room turned from bright and cheery to dull and gloomy in a matter of seconds. Despite the bright pink walls, my room looked like a dark abyss.

శ్రీశ్రీ

That night, after Mom went to bed, I snuck outside to the back deck. I sat on the bench seat and looked up at the stars. Soft tinkling sounds from the wind chime filled the empty backyard. I really wanted to talk to Mrs. V. For as long as I could remember, she was always there for me. If I'd gone to her with this problem, she would've known just what to say over a cup of hot chocolate with marshmallows. Then she would've smoothed my hair and given me a hug. That was the thing with Mrs. V. She knew that some things were unfixable, but the right words could sooth the pain.

I sighed and my eyes filled with tears that spilled down my cheeks. I hated being so alone. No one to talk to. Then an idea crossed my mind. Maybe I could talk to Tamara and not worry about her getting hurt. I wouldn't tell her everything.

I hurried back inside and grabbed my phone from my

room. Once I was back outside, I sent a text to Tamara.

You still up? I asked. A few seconds passed.

Hey, girl! What's going on?

A lot…

What's wrong?

I'm missing Dad. And everyone.

How's Mrs. V?

She's still in the nursing home…still the same. I found a letter in Mom's room today.

Okaaaaay.

I took a deep breath and typed, *It was from Dad…for me. Mom never gave it to me.*

There was a long pause. *Why not?*

Not sure.

Are you going to ask her?

No.

Any more feelings of being watched?

My heart skipped a beat. She remembered our conversation. Should I tell her about the ghost? Should I tell her that it followed me? I sighed. No. I couldn't. So, I lied. *Not really.*

Good. I was starting to worry about your sanity!

The corners of my mouth turned up. It felt good to talk to Tamara again.

So much had happened that it felt like forever since I'd last talked to her. Tamara and I talked into the night. She took some weight from my sinking shoulders, so I could keep going.

ᑯᔆᑯ

The next evening, after more chores, I stood in the shower and let the water rinse away the dirt from the yard work. Grandma and Grandpa were coming Saturday.

A knock sounded at the door. "Honey?" Mom asked.

Since I had finished washing, I turned off the water, stepped out of the shower, and wrapped a towel around me. I cracked the door.

Mom stood with her neck craned toward the door. She said, "Your friends are here. They want you to go to the movies." Her voice was low, confidential. I sucked in a breath. Zane was here? "We need to talk about some things, but for tonight you can go. I've already told them to have a seat while you finish your shower."

Her words didn't really make sense at first. After last night, I thought she would be full of questions, not willing to let me out of her sight. Why would she be willing to let me go out? Of course, I wanted to go, but the movies were the last thing on my mind.

The idea of Zane waiting on me made my stomach flutter, but when I remembered the damage at the pier, it stopped. An image of the charred wood splintered upward was confirmed as a warning from the ghost not to get too close, that the ghost in the blue dress was growing more powerful.

At that moment, I realized that I not only feared the little ghost, but that I also resented her for what I had to do. "Tell them to go ahead without me. I still feel sick from yesterday."

"Oh, honey. What's wrong?" She started to push the bathroom door open, to come in and be my loving mother. But I pushed it closed, pushed her out, pushed her away.

"Nothing…well, I think it's a cold or something. My throat's sore and I think I have a fever," I said through the door.

When she walked away, I leaned my forehead against the door and swallowed the lump in my throat. I could hear her telling Zane, Samantha, and Trey that I didn't feel well. After they left, I went to my room to lie down for the rest of the evening. I missed everything so much it hurt. I missed Mrs. V. I missed Pepe. I missed Tamara. And now I missed Mom. And I wasn't sure I could take much more.

✌✍✌✍

Later that night in my bedroom, I imagined the feel of Zane's arms around me, comforting, protecting. I wish I could have gone with him. I stood and stared out my bedroom window with the lights out, watching the night and listening to the musical tinkle of the wind chimes.

The night breeze tickled my arms, and I wished he were actually here to keep me warm and maybe have my first kiss. After the day at the pier, I was surprised that he wanted to see me again. My thoughts drifted to the ghost. Where was her sister? What had happened to her?

I crossed my arms to keep them warm and leaned against the window frame. Zane probably sat with another girl at the movies tonight since I couldn't go. A pang of jealousy caught me off guard.

If I could be so jealous of a girl I didn't know, then how would I have been with a sister? What if Zane liked her better?

My face grew hot, and I turned away from the window. An unsettled feeling spread through me, an awareness that things were spiraling away from me.

As if the ghost had heard me, the wind chimes went silent and the air became heavy. Every sound stopped. A numbing panic spread through my limbs, like the day I witnessed her appearance at the top of the stairs. I backed away from the window. She was here.

The wind from the window picked up, making the curtains blow in the breeze. Suddenly, they surrounded me. Startled, I pushed against them, trying to escape, but I couldn't. I was enclosed in a curtain prison.

"Mom!" I screamed, but the fabric muffled my cry.

The wind increased, circling me, like I was standing in the middle of a vortex. Around and around I turned, pushing against the lace curtains, unable to find a way out.

I screamed again. Was she finally trying to kill me? Would I end up like Mrs. V?

My favorite yellow top twisted around my body, tight. Too tight. The wind increased, pulling my once favorite shirt even tighter around my lungs. I couldn't breathe. I couldn't scream. I was going to die. Terror streaked through me and around me, up and up into the vortex.

Lightheaded and dizzy, I saw an image of the ghost appear on the other side. As if the floor had vanished, I felt like I was falling. Falling through a tunnel. I closed my eyes, afraid of where I would land.

Finally, I hit something hard and flat. I opened my eyes. Light flooded the room. After I pulled the curtains away, I realized that I lay sprawled on the floor of my room in the middle of my torn curtains, rods sticking out at odd angles. Mom stood in my doorway, hair up in a ponytail and bags under her eyes, staring at me with a horrified look on her face.

Without a sound she turned and left, leaving me alone.

CHAPTER 18

The next morning, after Mom had helped me put my curtain rods back up, she went into the kitchen to start the roast. No questions. No questions because she couldn't handle the answers. She was nearing her breaking point. The problem was—I had already reached mine.

The morning passed without much conversation. Grandma and Grandpa were due to arrive at noon, and sure enough, the doorbell rang right on time.

"Come here, sweetness, and give your grandma a hug," Grandma Pearl said, slipping off her sandals.

She wrapped her arms around me and the familiar scent of White Diamonds filled my nostrils. Her fluffy white hair sprang back into place once she released me. Her white capris and black and white top matched her sandals. Perfection. That was my Grandma Pearl.

"Look at my little Jenna. Growing like a weed, ain't she?" Grandpa Russ said and gave me a hug. His glasses magnified the wrinkles around his eyes, giving him a droopy sad look even though he smiled.

He turned to Mom and wrapped her in his arms. After a few seconds, Mom sniffed. Grandpa mumbled something that sounded like, "It's okay, Debra honey. Everything's gonna work out."

I understood that Mom was going through a lot. But it would've been nice for someone to hug me and tell me that "everything's gonna work out," because things weren't looking good right now.

After their hug, Mom turned to me and said, "Jenna, honey. Could you get the roast out of the oven?" Her tears disappeared as she wiped them from her cheeks, like they were never there.

I went to the kitchen and opened the oven. The heat came out in waves, carrying with it a delicious aroma. My stomach growled. Roast was one of my favorites. Mom showed the rest of the house. The mashed potatoes, gravy, and corn were already done. Once the tour reached my room, the talking became more hushed. I strained to hear but couldn't.

"Jenna," Grandma said and walked into the kitchen. Mom started putting plates on the table. "How about we go into town later and pick out some paint for your room?"

My eyes widened and my heart jumped. "Thanks, Grandma!" I wanted to hug her, but I couldn't. I was taking the foil off the roast.

Maybe that's what they were talking about. Finally, I could get rid of that obnoxious pink, and sooner than I expected.

"And pick out a new bedspread while we're at it," Grandma continued. "A prettier one."

My excitement faded. I didn't want a new bedspread. I loved the one I had. Mrs. V gave it to me. Not sure what else to say, I just smiled.

"Dinner's ready," Mom said.

She took one plate at a time and dished up a helping of roast. When she finished, we sat at the small four-person table to eat lunch.

Afterward, Grandpa wanted to see the barn. "I had a horse when I was a kid," he said on our way out the sliding doors at the back of the house. When I opened the side door of the barn, he adjusted his glasses and stepped inside, taking a look around. "So'd your mom. Patches was his name." The warm air threatened to suffocate us, and I glanced at him, worried that the heat would bother him. "It's a bit small, but I think it'll work. So what kind of horse are you looking at?"

I shrugged. "Nothing right now. The fence needs replaced, so it'll be a while."

He frowned, and we walked outside to look at the fence. "You're right. Tell you what. I know a guy that can fix this right up," he said and turned to me. "S'all you need to worry about is getting the horse."

My heart jumped for the second time today. "Really!" I said and hopped up and down like a kid. "I can't wait." I wrapped him in a big hug. "Thanks, Grandpa!" I said against his soft fine hair.

He laughed, low and full of love. "You're welcome."

I couldn't believe it. It wouldn't be long before I had a horse. Maybe something would finally go right for me.

☙☙☙

Grandpa walked back to the house. I skipped. The fields surrounding the house turned into places to ride and so did our road. Did a horse need shoes to ride on a dirt road? Would the rocks hurt its feet? I didn't know but I'd have to find out.

Mom and Grandma glanced at me when I entered the kitchen.

I smiled and made my way to the bathroom. On the way back to the kitchen, I heard them whispering.

"I'm not sure what to *do* with Jenna," Mom said. Her voice slightly muffled. "I thought things would be better once we moved. New house and new people." My mother sighed. "Instead, they've gotten worse."

"You need to talk with her," Grandma said. "Teenagers are a hard group. I should know."

"I really don't know what to say to her or how to

bring it up. I've already told her that I want her to see a therapist."

I flinched. Hadn't she dropped that issue? Maybe she reconsidered when she found me on the floor all tangled up in my curtains.

Grandpa sighed. "I think you need to give her some time to adjust. *You* still haven't got things together, so why should she?"

Tears flooded my eyes, and I rested my head back against the wall. How could I face them? They were talking behind my back, not even an hour after my grandparents arrived. I trudged to my room, again—the dark abyss.

I plopped down on my bed and curled up on top of my beautiful bedspread. With my curtains back up, everything looked normal except for the pink walls, one streaked with deep purple. No evidence remained of the terror I felt last night.

Fresh air made its way through the open window. I breathed deeply, my ribs were still sore. I had been thinking of having a sister when it happened. Was there some type of connection?

While I stared at the ceiling, the hairs on my arms slowly stood on end and the air became heavier than before. No! The ghost was near, and I couldn't deal with that right now.

Things were out of control. A dream or two with visions of a little girl in a dress were nothing compared to

last night. Last night, I was in real danger. I almost suffocated.

I turned my head. She waited in the corner. Every
ounce of courage that I had was now gone, swallowed by
the spinning vortex.

I scrambled to my feet and rushed to the door. I tried
to open it but couldn't. Locked! It couldn't be. It didn't
even have a lock. I lost my grip on the doorknob and fell
backward. I glanced into the corner.

"Sissy?"

I couldn't move or breathe or look away. The blue of
the dress became a blur as it floated toward me, disorient-
ing me, causing me to see weird things.

Two little blonde girls played dolls together in the
kitchen of my old house, giggling. Their dresses were
similar to one another. One sister coughed, looked
around, and motioned to her throat. The other sister in the
blue dress stood, pushed a chair to the counter, and
grabbed a glass of what looked like water and handed it
to her sister to drink.

Their mother walked in, hair pulled into a high bun.
When she witnessed her daughter drinking from the
glass, she swatted it from her hand. The daughter looked
up, her face shrunken like a mummy. Empty eye sockets.

I screamed. Panic hit me in the chest, and I scrambled backward until I was against the wall. I blinked sev-
eral times. My vision cleared, and the ghosts disappeared.

"Jenna?" Mom asked outside my door.

"Mom!"

"Jenna!" Her voice sounded panicked, and she pushed the door open. Mom, Grandma, and Grandpa rushed into my room. I sat on the floor, my back against the wall.

"What's wrong?" Grandma asked and knelt down beside me, searching for the cause of my distress.

I glanced into the corner, searching for the little girl in the blue dress. I hoped this time someone else would see her too, but she was gone. Mom and Grandma exchanged a look, quick but there. Mom's was full of worry, but Grandma's was different. I couldn't figure it out at first. But when she turned to leave, I saw it again—disgust.

ഔഔഔ

Late Saturday evening, the sun began to set, casting a soft glow that reflected off the store windows on Main Street. We'd driven into town, all of us. Grandma Pearl kept my arm wrapped in hers while we strolled through the paint store. I wanted to buy a neutral paint and then visit Zane.

"Well, hello again," the sales lady said. "I wondered what happened to you the other day."

Grandma looked at me, eyebrows raised.

"It didn't quite work out as I had planned," I said.

The vivid image of purple water in the carpet shampooer popped into my mind. A moment of silence passed when I didn't explain. How could I? Something that only I could see tipped the paint over just because it could. No. It would be blamed on me, as usual. I didn't put the lids on tight enough.

The sales lady cleared her throat, and I glanced at Grandma. "How about we look at all the colors over here," Grandma said and walked over to the paint cards. "How about this one?" I shook my head. No more shades of purple. "No? How about this one?" She held out a pretty sage green that reminded me of Mom's room. I shook my head. A pale yellow caught my eye, and I picked it up. "You don't want yellow. It's too bright during the day. That's more for the kitchen, dear." I put it back.

Then I picked up a neutral tan. "This is it," I said. Neutral was what I wanted and it would go with my bedspread. "This one is perfect."

"Oh, dear. That isn't a very pretty color," Grandma said. Then she picked up a blue card. "I really like this shade here," she said and held out a very brilliant blue, similar to the shade of the ghost's dress. "I'm drawn to it. It would be beautiful." She grabbed my arm, consumed by her excitement.

Goosebumps started in the middle of my body and spread all the way down my arms and legs. Should I be afraid?

Had something else influenced her color choice? Just

the thought of having that color on my walls nauseated me.

"I don't like that color," I said.

"Well," Grandma said, raising her chin. She squinted her eyes at me. "Your mother was right. You are a difficult one."

I withdrew my arm from her tight grip. "I'm sorry, Grandma."

"Well you should be. I'm offering to buy new paint for your room, and you're being as finicky as a feline," she said and took out her flowered handkerchief. She dabbed the sweat from her forehead and upper lip and looked around with an aggravated expression.

"What's going on?" Mom asked with a can of stain for the deck in her hands.

"I can't get anywhere with Jenna here. None of these colors are good enough for her." Grandma lifted her chin again. "Not even this beautiful blue."

Mom shot me an angry look. "Jenna? Is this true?"

"But, Mom—"

"I can't believe this, young lady." Mom continued. "I didn't raise you to be this…this…ungrateful spoiled little brat!" She grabbed Grandma's arm, and they turned and left. Then Grandpa left. I looked to the sales lady to try to explain, but she left, too.

I stood alone surrounded by hundreds of different colors. I held up the blue paint card still in my hand. Out of all those colors, my Grandma picked this one. What was I going to do? I couldn't keep going like this. My eyes filled with tears, and it felt like the dark abyss had followed me all the way to town. I didn't want to cry. Not here, not now. I ducked my head and started toward the restroom.

Once inside, I shut the door and locked it. I slid down into a sitting position, and the tears fell. My mother's words echoed in my head. *Spoiled little brat.* While I stared at the paint card in my hand, an awful feeling built inside me. Finally, I couldn't stand it anymore. I kicked the metal trash can. The sound echoed in the small cement room, and I liked it. I kicked it again. This time my foot left a small dent in the side.

I stared at the dent, savoring the fact that I'd just damaged something on purpose. It felt good. It took the edge off the awful feeling that had spread through my insides. I'd never experienced these intense feelings before.

Anger at my mother. Anger at my grandma. And most of all, anger at the ghost in the blue dress. What did she want from me? I ripped the paint card in half, then in half again, then I ripped each little piece in half until it looked like it had been put through the shredder. I let them fall from my fingers, just like the tears falling from my cheeks.

CHAPTER 19

After what seemed like an eternity, I finally opened the door to the restroom. The store was empty and so was the TrailBlazer. They must've gone into the antique store across the street, so I headed toward the Pizza Shop, just to see Zane or maybe Trey and Samantha.

I took a deep breath of fresh air and hoped that my face didn't look too puffy from crying. The wind blew my long brown hair around my shoulders, and I brushed it back before opening the door to the restaurant. My shirt and shorts looked plain compared to the other kids hanging out. But I didn't care. I wanted to see Zane.

He had just taken an order when he noticed me standing at the door. He smiled and nodded toward an empty booth in the far corner. I hurried over and sat to wait. I felt important, seeing him rush through the orders, so he could come see me. Of course, I had crushes at my old school, but I'd never felt like this. And I liked it.

He smiled and sat. "I only have a minute to talk. They called me in tonight because one of the waiters called in sick. Must be something going around. How are you feeling?"

For a second, I didn't know what he meant, but then I remembered not going to the movies with him. "I feel a lot better, thanks. I only have a minute, too. I'm in town with Mom and my grandparents."

"Are you ready for school Tuesday?"

I shrugged. "As ready as I'll ever be." School was the last thing on my mind right now.

"You're not nervous?"

"Not really. I've been a little too busy lately to think about it."

He smiled his dazzling white smile and his blue eyes mesmerized me for a moment. Only for a moment did they remind me of the color of the dress in the fading light of the evening. And only for a moment did I think I was wrong in wanting and deserving to be normal and have normal friends. He leaned close and put his hand over mine.

"You're probably not worried because you know I'll be there." His voice low, intimate. The warmth of his touch was more than comforting.

It was a link to being normal. Something I hadn't had

for so long, I'd forgotten what it felt like. But when the air changed, heavy and electric, I jerked my hand away. And just at that moment, the front door opened. Mom and Grandma walked in.

At first there was confusion in Zane's eyes, quickly followed by understanding. *Yes. Please think Mom and Grandma walking in was the reason I pulled away. Not something else, something only I can see, something Dad had tried to warn me about.*

Heat spread through my cheeks. Didn't they see the invisible sign I'd hung on the door that said no parents or grandparents allowed?

Zane stood and gave me a wink. "I'd better get back to work."

"Jenna, we're ready to go," Grandma said in her curt voice and walked out. A dangerous heaviness still hung in the air. I inched my way out of the booth, my legs sticking to the vinyl seat.

A quick glance around the room showed no little blue dress or glowing red eyes. I wasn't sure of her capabilities, but then I never had been. Between the lightning at the pier and tipping my paint over, I knew she could follow me. I needed to be more careful.

*დ*დ*დ*

By the time Sunday evening rolled around, Grandma and Grandpa were gone, along with their promises of paint, a new bedspread, and most importantly a new fence. They didn't say anything more about it when they left last night. I just gave them both a hug before they walked out the front door. Tonight, I just wanted to be alone for once, to think about everything that had happened.

To think about Dad.

To think about Mrs. V and Pepe.

And, to think about Zane.

I put the mayonnaise back in the fridge, grabbed my sandwich, and headed out to the deck. The sun decided to hide behind a cloud when I took my seat on the glider bench, casting the deck in shadows. Goosebumps popped up on my arms but disappeared once the cloud passed.

I soaked up the warmth and listened to the wind chime's sad song while I ate. I thought about the ghost and her sister. If I had a sister, we'd definitely fight over clothes and boys. That was for sure. But we would've still loved each other—no matter what.

The French doors opened. Thinking it was Mom, I continued eating my sandwich. But it was Samantha and Trey. My pulse sped up, and I sat a little straighter, looking for Zane. But he didn't come. I wanted to ask about him, but sensed I shouldn't. Maybe it was Samantha's red and swollen eyes.

Neither one would look at me. My sandwich still hung midway to my mouth. No air had moved in or out of my lungs.

Sam cleared her throat and looked at Trey. He shook his head and looked down at his feet. Finally Sam blurted out, "Zane's been in a car accident."

All feeling left my body, and I dropped my turkey sandwich. It hit the side of my leg before falling to the floor.

Trey looked up for a moment and then resumed looking at his shoes. "They say he's going to be all right, but it was pretty bad."

I couldn't speak.

"He was on his way to a party," Sam said, her voice wasn't so shrill and annoying right now, "when he lost control and hit a telephone pole on his side of the car."

I couldn't breathe.

"We just thought you should know."

Trey finally met my eyes and then a moment later Samantha did, but I had to look away. I couldn't look them in the eye, knowing that the ghost in the blue dress was most likely the cause of this.

Would I ever know for sure?

But the warning at the pier was her, without a doubt. I'd felt her presence. And I'd felt her presence at the Pizza Shop.

The feel of his hand on mine, the feel of being normal for a few minutes, all of that wasn't worth the feeling of being the one responsible.

They left without saying anything more. They couldn't manage it, and neither could I.

eↄeↄ

"What did your friends have to say?" Mom walked out onto the deck and closed the French doors. When she saw me picking up my sandwich, she became still. I put my plate with the ruined turkey in the empty seat next to me, hoping she would take the hint and leave. I needed to be alone.

I turned my face away from her and watched the corn in the neighboring field sway in the breeze. Another moment passed. Her footsteps came toward me. I felt her hands around my cheeks, turning me to face her.

"What's *wrong*?" Her voice broke. "Talk-to-me!" She emphasized each word.

"I can't."

"Yes, you can! Now talk to me. What's going on here?"

"I can't." My voice started to shake and so did my heart. I wanted so bad to confide in her. I wanted someone else to help me. But I knew I couldn't. She'd end up like Mrs. V and now Zane. "Believe me, Mom. I can't."

And with that I broke down. My tears soaked into her shirt, and she wrapped her arms around me. Rocking me, soothing me, loving me. Just like when I was little.

CHAPTER 20

That night, I withdrew to my room, Roscoe and my comforter by my side. I sighed, exhausted. Everything seemed to blur together now. I just wanted to sleep and to forget. But just as I was lying down, the air became heavy and the curtains stopped moving, as if the ghost had been waiting and listening for her moment.

All of my moments had turned to *her* moment. When I confided in Mrs. V, she took her away from me. When I got too close to Zane, she took him away from me, too. I was so tired of not knowing what she wanted from me.

I did know one thing I wanted. I wanted her gone. Forever. My head hurt and my stomach ached from the guilt and knowledge that I might have caused Zane's accident. If only I hadn't gone to the Pizza Shop.

I glanced around my room, looking for her in the corner, but she wasn't there. I glanced at the window. Not there either. Well, then where was she? I leaned up, searching. There she sat at the foot of my bed with a smile on her face, kicking her feet like an excited child.

My heart jumped into my throat, and adrenaline burned through my body. She'd never been so close. At first, numbness started spreading through my body, fear taking over. But I stopped it, replacing it with something else. The feeling I had when I kicked that trash can in the paint store over and over.

It was like all of the fear molecules were changing to rage molecules, colliding into one another until they merged into one great emotion that I couldn't explain. It built, built, built until I couldn't stand it.

I lunged, arms wide, hands ready.

I wanted to catch the ghost in the blue dress and physically harm her. I wanted to curse her and send her away. Away from me and everyone I loved.

But she was too fast. I landed on my chest with my arms out, bouncing just enough that I bumped my forehead on the bedpost. My head stung. I sprang from my bed, crouched, ready to spring again. I wanted to destroy her.

I searched my room, chest heaving. But I didn't see her anywhere. Not in the corner. Not by the window. And not on my bed.

She was gone.

I paced my room, daring her to come back. I yanked at my curtains.

"Come on, ghost," I said low and quiet. Taunting. I paced my room some more. With each lap, the adrenaline began to fade. My breathing began to even out. And I seriously began to doubt my sanity.

After an hour or so, I sat on the edge of my bed. Physically and emotionally spent, I curled up on my side. With Roscoe held tight, the tears started to come, slowly at first, then a steady stream. I was so tired of crying.

A little later into the night, when I was just about asleep, electricity returned to the air. I stiffened and waited. I didn't wait long, though. The ghost appeared right in front of me, staring directly into my eyes. I jerked back.

Her bright blue form jumped up and down as if she were an excited little child. Quickly, I pulled my arm out from under my blanket and swiped at her. I wanted to hurt her.

My hand and fingers moved through her bright form as if I were pulling my hand through water. I watched her colors swirl together but not quite mixing. They stayed separate, coming back together only when I had finished pulling my hand through.

In the second that it took for my hand to swipe through her, her excited expression changed into something else. I pulled back. The ghost quickly faded but not before I saw what her expression had changed into.

Grief.

❡❡❡

The next day, I looked in the mirror at the lump on my forehead. It was even bigger and bluer than the last time I'd looked at it, a reminder of last night's drama. Zane was on my mind just like Mrs. V. And tomorrow was the first day of school.

Frustrated, I grabbed my foundation and dabbed some on the lump, but it didn't look right. Maybe concealer would work better. That's what I needed. I went to Mom's bathroom, searched through her wicker makeup basket, and found it. I dabbed it on my forehead.

I checked the bump again. Now it looked like I had a pigmentation problem because Mom's makeup appeared lighter than my skin. I rummaged through the basket and found some bronzer. Using the round sponge, I dabbed it on, smoothing it over my face. Much better. Now a little blush. Perfect.

Why should I even worry? Zane wouldn't be there. I pushed the awful thought to the back of my mind. When I replaced the brush, I saw the reflection of Mom's bedroom in the mirror, door slightly ajar.

I thought of the letter Dad wrote for me that she didn't want me to see. I should return it while I had the chance. I hurried to my room and grabbed the envelope. Once I made it back to Mom's room, I unlocked the cedar chest, pulled out the picture album, and slid the envelope back inside. When I put the album back, I pulled a section of Mom's wedding dress to cover it. And when I did, I saw a small box wrapped in birthday paper with a small silver bow tucked in the corner. I picked it up.

It was the size of a Precious Moments figurine for my sixteenth birthday from Dad.

CHAPTER 21

Tuesday morning, the first day of school, and I had no idea what to wear. Plus the bump on my forehead had turned a darker shade of blue. Great. I hoped the concealer and bronzer held up. I tossed yet another shirt over my shoulder and proceeded to another. The most important thing was to not get too close to anyone else again. At least until I'd figured out how to destroy the ghost.

When the bus rolled up, I grabbed my bag. Mom gave me a hug and a kiss. "Have a good day, honey. See you tonight."

After the ride to school, I stepped off the bus and took a deep breath.

Maybe I'd see Samantha and Trey. But did I really want to? Would they see how guilty I felt and wonder what was going on? Or would they just assume that I was upset?

I walked along the sidewalk under the awning toward the front doors. Others bustled by me, knowing where they were going. I took my time, not wanting to sit by myself for long in my first class. I stepped through the front doors and the artificial lights took over.

Once I walked farther down the hall on my way to my locker, I saw Samantha. "Hey, Sam," I said.

"Hey!" She gave me a small smile and glanced at my forehead.

"Long story," I said and shrugged. "So—how's Zane?"

"Better." She nodded, her lips a thin line. "The doctor said he fractured his left arm and they put a cast on it yesterday—then they sent him home." When she said that last word, she went up on her toes, bringing my spirits up with her. She must have read that in my expression, because she broke out into a huge smile. The dull ache in my chest loosened a little with the good news. "He'll wear a cast for a few weeks but should be back to school soon. He's really sore."

"I'm so glad to hear that he's okay," I said in a rush. "Please tell him that I said 'Hi' and that I'm sorry."

"Will do—so what's your first class?" She kicked her locker shut with her heel. She had an over-sized Chemistry book in her arms.

"Algebra."

"Yuck. The classroom's down that hall." She tilted her head to the right. "I've got Chemistry down this hall." She tilted her head in the other direction. "Otherwise, I'd show ya. Meet me here at my locker at lunch time, so we can sit together."

"Okay." I made my way in the opposite direction, searching for my classroom, wondering how to get out of becoming friends with Sam.

∾∾∾

I was still debating what to do when I walked into class late.

"Name?"

The voice startled me, and I looked to the front of the room. The teacher, a mid-forties man standing with his back to a large white board, stared back at me. Gray lightly peppered his receding hairline, almost the same color as his tie. He looked like a teacher that I didn't want as an enemy.

I remembered he asked me my name. "Jenna Moores."

"Take a seat, Jenna. Not many left to choose from." He looked to the back of the room. I headed for the nearest desk. It sat next to a girl who had long, dark hair and heavy dark eyeliner. The slightly red lipstick complimented her dark skin tone but wasn't overboard. No one else sat near her.

As if she knew I wondered about her, she leaned over and whispered. "I'm Katrina. You can call me Kat."

I smiled and waved my hand, silently saying 'Hi.' Her friendly expression changed when her gaze shot behind me.

I turned around, hoping that someone else was late, so I wouldn't be the bad student so soon. Only I didn't see anyone. I turned back to Kat. She had her book open, and her hair pulled to the side, making a shield between us.

I looked behind me again. Nothing. But when I opened my book, I felt the change in the air.

ᗑᏽᗑ

At lunchtime, I went to the office. I didn't feel well. And the truth was, I really didn't. After a few questions from the secretary, I finally got to lie down in the sick room on a small cot. This was the only thing I could think of to avoid sitting with Samantha at lunch.

The nurse disposed of the little plastic cover and put the thermometer away. "You don't have a fever, Jenna."

"Really? Well…it's more of a headache than anything," I said, trying to get her to leave me alone. "Maybe if I just rest for lunch, I'll be okay."

This seemed to satisfy her, and she turned off the light and closed the door. The darkness didn't bother me. Night or day, it didn't matter. The ghost was always there, from the old house to the new, from home to school, it didn't matter. The ghost had attached itself to me somehow, and I didn't want anyone else to get hurt.

Just as I started to relax and almost fall asleep, a bell rang, startling me. Lunch period was over already. My stomach growled, and I sat up and gathered my bag. They said Mrs. V had a stroke and that Zane had a car accident, but I knew it was the ghost in the blue dress. What if she was too strong for me to destroy? Maybe it was time to give up. I didn't need friends anyway.

The nurse popped her head into the room. "Feeling any better?"

"Not really."

കൗൽ

That night, I couldn't sleep. A cool breeze came through my window, bringing with it the promise of rain. I inhaled deeply, hoping the deep cleansing breath would help me relax. It didn't. My curtains moved in rhythm with my breathing. A slow inhale brought them toward me, and then a slow exhale pushed them away, the movement slight, but there. I watched, creating my own little game. Slowly, I drifted into a dream...

കൗൽ

I could hear the rumble of tires. I could see the car.

Zane driving down a back road, radio up, on his way to the party.

Just seeing him fueled my guilt. The words he'd said to me at the Pizza Shop. "I bet you're not nervous, because I'll be there." Then there was the wish to be normal and to have friends.

Something bright. Lightning flashed, striking a front tire. He lost control and veered right. He tried to regain control by yanking the steering wheel left, but it only caused the car to slide and fishtail. The driver's side of the car slid into a telephone pole, hitting his door and smashing his window. When he finally stopped, his body was limp. Blood ran from a gash in the top of his forehead. He didn't move.

ℰℑℰℑ

The dream ended. I blinked to clear my mind. The bedroom came back into focus just in time to see headlights bounce off my walls, and off the ghost standing in the middle of my room. A sick feeling rose in my gut. Now I knew for sure the lightning was her, just like at the pier.

After last night, I didn't care about my under eye circles or humungous bump on my forehead, which got a quizzical look from Kat. She didn't say anything. In fact, she turned her attention away from me. For a moment, I thought she might get up and change seats, but she didn't.

The bell rang, and we all opened our books while the teacher started his lecture on finding X. Finding X was important to him, but finding out how to destroy the ghost in the blue dress was more important to me, especially after last night.

But how? How did I destroy her? What was keeping her here? I learned yesterday that she followed me to school. And I knew she was powerful, and I knew she was dangerous. How did I destroy a ghost like that? The only logical thing I could think of was the dress. Even though it was mine, she was connected to it. She had to be. Why else was she wearing it?

The window on the other side of the room was more interesting than the teacher, raindrops chasing each other until they hit the bottom. Today was a dark, gloomy, awful day, which turned out to match my mood perfectly.

"Jenna?" Everyone turned their attention to the back of the room where I sat. I stiffened in my chair and felt blood rush to my face. The teacher stared at me. "Did you even hear the question?"

I bit my lower lip, hard, just about ready to confess when Kat whispered the answer. I cleared my throat. "Two positives?"

He narrowed his eyes at me as if he knew I had help. Point proven. He went on. I lowered my head, trying to hide my embarrassment from everyone around, including myself.

When the lecture ended, we had a few minutes before the bell. I turned to Kat. "Thanks," I said and closed my book.

"No problem." She wouldn't look at me as she gathered her things. And before I could say another word, she left.

෧෩෩

That night I sat at my desk, facing the wall, trying to concentrate on my homework. The rain came down in an unsteady rhythm with water trickling down the gutter pipe. The wind blew the rain against my window in waves, harder for a bit then it would lessen, as if it was over, only to start again. The room was dark except for a desk lamp shining directly on my algebra book.

I twirled a loose strand of hair around my finger, the rest up in a messy ponytail. Mom had already gone to bed, and I was getting tired. But I had to finish my homework for tomorrow, something I had saved for last.

Last night's dream weighed on my mind. I scribbled an answer that looked like it might be right. In the back of my mind, I waited for her to show up. She was here. I could feel it. Just three more problems to solve, then I could try to get to bed without seeing her. My eyelids started to droop.

A yawn escaped followed by a nod of my head. X started to blur into Y until I really couldn't tell a difference. Finally, I gave up and dropped my pencil. I rubbed my eyes and then turned toward the window. Something moved. I rolled my computer chair a little closer. There were figures moving in the glass, like a TV show in my window. I gasped and rubbed my eyes again.

One of the figures was the ghost in the blue dress. She stood in the doorway of my old room watching her mother and a man who looked like a doctor. The ghost glanced back over her shoulder, making sure I was watching. The mother and doctor stood over another little girl, the one that looked just like her. Her twin.

A moment later, the doctor looked up at the mother and slowly shook his head. His gaze returned to the sick little girl before he reached up and gently closed her eyelids.

The mother dropped to her knees and threw back her head, letting out a silent wail. The ghost in the blue dress turned and ran, her wavy hair bouncing behind her. She ran out of the window and into my room, but she didn't stop. She just kept going, going as if I weren't there, disappearing into the wall just as the scene on my window vanished.

I rolled my chair back to my desk and sat there, silent, stunned. Silent because of the horror I had just witnessed and stunned that she had shown me this in my window. How strong was she? Afraid of the answer, I tried to remember the images instead.

Her twin sister had died. I could understand that much. But if her twin sister had died at such a young age, then why was she so young? Did she die of the same thing? Now I had even more questions than before.

So I reached up to turn off the desk lamp. Just as I flipped the switch, I heard something. Quickly I turned back to the window, thinking there was more to be seen. Instead, it was dark. Then I heard the noise again.

A child screaming.

CHAPTER 22

The next morning, I took my seat next to Kat. When I glanced over, she was busy working on something with her book open. I gasped. My assignment! Too tired last night, I didn't finish. I opened my book and pulled out the piece of paper from last night. My intentions were to get in here early to get it done.

Frantically, I worked the next problem. Done. Now the next. The teacher walked into the room and sat at his desk. Done. Now the next one. I looked up again and met his stare. He smiled and stood. "All right, class. Pass your homework up. Anything turned in after this will be counted as late."

"Thirty-four," Kat whispered. I gave her a questioning look. "The last one on your homework—thirty-four."

Hurrying, I wrote the answer and passed it to the person in front of me. "Thanks."

I wanted to talk with her more, but knew I shouldn't. And my guess was that she knew she shouldn't either. When I glanced over, she had her head down, concentrating on her algebra with her hair in a long, black curtain between us. The idea that she might have seen something yesterday comforted me. At the same time, though, it scared me. I didn't want another person getting hurt.

❧❦❧

After school, I walked to the library. I didn't want to go home. There was nothing there. The sun finally decided to come out from behind two days' worth of rain clouds. The summer heat seemed to magnify every time I took a step, but I didn't slow down. I was tired of letting the ghost ruin my life. I was going to take control. Otherwise, I would be stuck with a dangerous ghost and no friends and no family.

The air conditioning rolled over me like an invisible wall when I opened the door to the library. I hadn't realized how humid it really was outside. My hair had to be a wild mess by now. Not that I cared at this moment. I was here to find a way to destroy the ghost in the blue dress.

Once I searched the library catalog, I sat at a corner table, away from everyone else. I looked at the empty chair sitting next to me and wished Pepe were here. I missed him so much. I hoped he was doing okay with Jessica and the kids. I'd call this evening and check on him and Mrs. V. Tell Jessica that everything was just fine here.

The first book looked helpful but really wasn't. The cover was black, white, and gray with the letters written in a bright red cursive. It was filled with folklore from Dracula to werewolves. If only it were that easy. Drive a wooden stake through the ghost's heart or shoot her with a silver bullet.

I would gladly take my pick. But so far I wasn't having any luck.

I picked up another book and flipped through the aged pages. The edges were uneven, cut purposefully to look older than it was. Still, nothing interesting or helpful. Then I caught a glimpse of someone approaching my table. Quickly I flipped my book over, hoping they didn't see what I was reading.

When I glanced up, I saw the person was Kat, the look on her face strained as if she were concentrating. She didn't make eye contact either, but when she reached my side, she slid a book onto my table and made sure it was open before she left. No words or anything to communicate her intentions.

That's weird. But when I looked at the book in front of me, I knew exactly what she intended. She was helping me. Frantically, I read the paragraphs and studied the pictures listed. She had brought me the book I needed, the

one I had been searching for. It was about real-life en-
counters with ghosts and how to destroy them.

‽‽

I didn't realize how late it was when I finished reading the information I needed. I had to call Mom.

"Where are you?" She didn't even try to control the
sharp edge to her voice.

"At the library."

"Why didn't you call me at work and let me know
what you were doing?"

"I didn't think about it."

"You didn't think about letting me know that you
wouldn't be home when I got here?"

"I'm sorry, Mom. Really. I just lost track of time. I
had to do some research for school."

She paused. For a moment, I wondered if she believed me or not. She sighed. "I'll be there as soon as I
can," she said and hung up, the tone of her voice enough
to tell me that I was in trouble. Was it worth it? Yes.

Now I needed to figure out for sure what the link
was. What kept the ghost connected to this world and to
me? The dress had to have something to do with it. But
why would my dress be the link for the ghost?

A little while later, lost in my reasoning, I didn't hear
the footsteps behind me. "Jenna?" It was Mom. I turned
around. "I've been waiting outside for five minutes." The

artificial light of the library accented her puffy eyes and the wrinkles on her forehead. For the first time, I could actually see that she'd aged this summer.

I stood and grabbed my bag. "Sorry, Mom," I said, but she had already turned, heading back out the double doors of the library to the car.

On our way home, she didn't say a word. I wanted her to yell at me, scold me, anything just so I'd know that she would be okay, that we were going to be okay. But she didn't.

When we pulled into the garage, she turned off the engine and got out. She opened the garage door, walked into the kitchen, and shut the door, leaving me sitting— alone.

৩৯৫৩

I sat in my room that night, working on my homework, but I couldn't stop staring at the wall, bouncing my pencil off my chin. Something had to be done about the ghost and soon. Even though I wasn't sure the dress was the link, my plan was to burn it. But when?

Tomorrow.

Just as my thoughts shifted to the ghost, the air became heavy and electric, more so than the previous nights. Something was different, and I didn't like it. I looked at the window. No figures in the reflection. I looked in the corners. No blue dress.

The air became so heavy, it pushed me into my chair. The scream that I had heard the other night echoed within my room. I tried to stand, to leave this awful mess that she'd made, but couldn't. My head became so heavy I could barely hold it up. I had to lower it onto my desk and close my eyes. Instead of escaping, I was right in the middle of everything…

ᕽᕽᕽ

The doorway to my old room stood open. I watched the ghost's mother and the old doctor care for the sick twin sister. The ghost in the blue dress was only a small child, but the look on her face said she understood what was happening. She understood something was very wrong with her sister, her friend, her other half.

When the doctor shook his head and the mother began to wail, the ghost in the blue dress turned and ran. Her little black shoes pounded the hardwood floor. She raced along the hallway. It was the last vision I'd seen last night. But there was more to be seen. She slowed down when she neared the balcony.

Somehow I understood that the sisters would crawl to the edge on their tummies and peek over the edge, holding each other's hand so they felt safe.

"Now you two be careful," the mother had said. "It's dangerous."

A breeze, cool against my arms and cheeks, rushed

down the hall. The faint silhouette of the twin sister who had just died moments earlier flew up and over the railing, gracefully dipping and diving in the empty space above the living room.

The ghost in the blue dress called out, "Sissy!"

I watched her place her tiny hands on top of the railing of the second-story balcony and climb. With a firm grip on the banister, she slowly stood, teetering just a little until she regained her balance.

"Sissy, wait for me!"

The twin sister saw the ghost in the blue dress standing on the banister and stopped dipping and diving. The twin sister brightened, floated closer, and closer and held out her hand.

The ghost in the blue dress reached for it, teetering on the balcony.

"Don't!" I yelled.

But it was too late. The ghost's foot slipped on the polished wood of the second-story balcony. Her little hands reached out, scrambling for anything to hold on to, but she lost her grip and fell to the floor below.

⸎⸎⸎

The silent thud of her body woke me. I jerked my eyes open, the thud sounding over and over and over in my head.

Carefully, I peeled the stuck algebra page from my

cheek and straightened. I looked at the clock. Midnight. I rolled my head from side to side and sat for a moment, collecting myself. The image of the little girl falling to her death haunted me, playing repeatedly in my mind. The realization was slow. I was so used to seeing her in the blue dress that it took me a moment to process it.

The little ghost died in a blue dress. And so did her twin.

I climbed into bed, pulled my pink comforter up to my chin, and held Roscoe close. I closed my eyes, drained. Sounds of a child crying, deep uncontrollable sobbing, came quietly from within my room. So real. So filled with pain and longing swirled together with no way to separate them. Then a tear slid out of the corner of my eye, quickly soaked up by Roscoe.

ɞɷɞɷ

The next morning, I stayed home. I didn't feel well. Mom didn't argue. She took my temperature and then left for work. When she was gone, I made my way into the kitchen. A note on the counter said there was sandwich meat in the refrigerator for lunch. I tromped around a little and decided to make some coffee.

The smell took me back. Dad sitting at the table, drinking his morning cup, cream and a little sugar. I never really paid attention to the details before he got sick. Now that he was gone, I found myself grasping at each memory and holding it tight, afraid I'd forget. And never remember again.

By the time I drank my coffee with hazelnut creamer, it was late morning. I'd been waiting to call Jessica and ask about Mrs. V and Pepe. So much had happened since the last time I'd seen Jessica, that I could hardly believe it. The thing was, it hadn't even been a month yet.

She answered after a few rings. "Jenna! How *are* you?"

"I'm okay," I said. "How's everybody there?"

"Mom's the same, holding on at the nursing home. You'll have to visit when you can."

"I'd like that." A moment of silence hung between us before I went on. "School's okay here."

Jessica paused a moment. "That's good, dear."

My breath caught and I couldn't speak for a second. Her voice. The way she said that sentence. She sounded just like Mrs. V and it hurt.

"Jenna? You still there?"

I sighed. She must've read into that sigh, because she couldn't say anything either for a little bit. She sniffed and blew her nose.

Once I felt collected enough to go on, I cleared my throat. "I'm sorry. I shouldn't have bothered you."

She laughed, a soft chuckle. "You're not bothering me. I want you to promise you'll call whenever you want, anytime. I know we don't know each other as well as we should, but you meant a lot to Mom." She sniffed again.

A tissue rattled against the phone. "So that means you're important to me, too."

I couldn't help the tears this time. This time her words hit me in the heart. She was taking care of me, just like Mrs. V.

"Thanks."

"No problem, kiddo. And guess what? Pepe's wagging his tail like crazy. I swear that dog's psychic."

I burst out laughing. "I think so, too! It's like he knows what you're thinking and everything."

We laughed together for a moment. A moment shared that would never be forgotten. Pepe barked and barked when Jessica held the phone down so he could hear my voice. I laughed some more.

Jessica and I talked for a little bit longer. I think she could tell I was having a hard time with everything—the move, missing Mrs. V and Pepe. Before we hung up, she invited me to come visit over fall break.

I told her I'd ask Mom and that I'd call again. After we hung up, my shoulders started to sag along with my spirits. I didn't realize how much I needed that talk and I didn't realize how much I needed that connection to Pepe and Mrs. V. And after last night's dream, I didn't realize how much I needed to be reminded that this was real.

Mrs. V hadn't recovered. I needed to destroy the ghost in the blue dress. Even though the ghost died accidently, even though she didn't know I wasn't her sister, she was still dangerous.

CHAPTER 23

After I'd finished my coffee at the small four-person kitchen table, I stood and put my cup in the dishwasher. I'd stayed home today, because now I knew the blue dress had to be the link. The ghost died in one, and so did her twin. So if I burned the dress, the ghost would be destroyed.

I did feel sorry for the little ghost. She'd lost her sister and then accidentally fell to her death. My scalp and arms tingled at the thought and my heart beat faster. I took a deep breath, commanding my heart to slow down. There was no apparent reason to panic—yet. I turned and walked out of the kitchen and down the hall, toward Mom's bedroom.

Now that I saw how the ghost had died and that she'd died wearing a little blue dress, I knew for sure that it had to be the link. And it was time that I burned that little thing to ashes.

Once I walked through the door, I stopped. Where could it be? I pictured Mom crushing it to her chest when she walked out of my bedroom door only two weeks ago. Two weeks? It seemed more like an eternity.

I started opening her dresser drawers and going through her things. No guilt or embarrassment slowed me down this time. Next drawer. Nothing. I rifled through her underwear drawer next. I found a picture of her and Dad when they first started dating. Dad looked directly into the camera, in love and healthy.

When I didn't find the dress in any drawer, I turned to the closet. It had to be in there. It wasn't in the cedar chest and not in her dresser drawers. It was the only logical place left. But just when I opened the door, the air became heavy, electric. This was even more intense than the last time. Maybe I was getting close! I reached up to the top shelf and pulled everything down into a heaping mess.

Quickly, I started rummaging. The hair on my arms stood up. I threw a couple high school yearbooks off to the side along with her varsity jacket. I moved on to the next box, but before I could pull the first thing out, the yearbook smacked me in the back of the head and fell to the ground. Stunned, I turned around.

The alarm clock floated in the air just inches above Mom's nightstand, ready to pummel me when the ghost gave the orders. Over on the other side of her room, her jewelry box floated, wavering up and down—waiting.

On the right a picture frame floated. Item by item rose into the air, her Precious Moments figurines, the afghan folded neatly on the cedar chest, and every item that I'd just thrown out of the first box.

Suddenly, Mom's childhood jewelry box that her grandma had given her came flying at me. I ducked. It hit the wall beside my head. A hairbrush flew at me but missed. I scrambled to my feet and raced toward the bedroom door with my arms and hands outstretched as a shield. But when I was just about there, it slammed shut. I was cornered.

I felt something grab my hair. It took me a second to realize it was the ghost. She started pulling my hair so hard that I lost my balance and fell to the floor. Then she smacked me in the face, one blow right after the other, like she was throwing a paranormal temper tantrum. I huddled in the fetal position on the floor with my arms protecting my head as if I were at school during a tornado drill. Suddenly, just as quickly as it started, everything stopped.

When a moment passed and nothing happened, I lowered my arms. The room looked like a real tornado had gone through it. The fact that the only injury I had sustained was the blow to the back of my head was unbelievable.

I brought myself to a sitting position and rubbed the

back of my head. A dull ache started at the base of my neck.

Anxious to leave, I staggered to my feet. The quilt on mom's bed began to move. It lifted in the middle, forming a tent. I had no idea what she was up to now, but I didn't want to stick around and find out.

I rushed to the door to open it, to finally leave, but it wouldn't budge. The door handle turned in my hand as I twisted it back and forth, but the door stuck, glued shut.

When I glanced behind me, I saw the quilt float off the bed and come toward me, similar to the wall of dark clouds at the lake. I sucked in a breath and turned back to the door.

I pulled the door handle again and again and again, but it wouldn't budge. Finally, I found my voice and screamed. Even though I knew Mom wasn't home, I screamed again. It was the only thing I could do. I was trapped.

The edge of the quilt touched my shoulder. I lashed out, turning and punching, but it didn't help. The quilt wrapped around me, like my curtains did before, and squeezed.

Not even an hour earlier, I had felt sorry for the ghost, for the loss of her sister and how she died. I even felt guilty for wanting to destroy her. But I was wrong, because now she was going to destroy me.

ေၺေၺ

I sat on the floor across from the ghost in the blue dress, her wavy hair pulled up in two high pigtails. She brushed her doll's hair with a little metal comb. She looked up at me, her eyes shimmering, and smiled. "Sissy. Play with me."

A doll of my own sat on my lap. When I reached over and picked up a hair bow to wrap around its hair, I saw my hand. Shocked, I pulled it back. It was small, like hers, and so were my feet and legs. I reached up and felt my hair. Pigtails. I wasn't fifteen anymore. I was a four-year-old in a matching blue dress.

But I wasn't afraid. Instead, I wanted to cry. I wanted to sob in Mommy's arms until the despair faded away, but she wasn't here.

I was alone.

Except for the ghost.

Did she win? Was I now a ghost, too? Again, I should've been afraid but the anguish and despair were all I felt.

How long had she been a ghost? I remembered the woman and doctor. It had to be a long time.

I don't want to spend eternity like this. Overwhelming emotions surged through me. Sadness, loneliness, confusion. I should've wanted to run. To fight. But I couldn't. The feelings from the ghost were too strong.

She was going to keep me here forever.

So I sat, playing with one doll, then another, wiping tiny tears from my face. The ghost handed me a tea cup with a saucer beneath it and pretended to pour some tea. But she must have run out, because she took the lid off the tea kettle and shrugged as if to say "No more." She stood, smoothing the ruffles of her dress like a young lady, and left.

The crippling feelings left me as soon as she was gone, and I could actually think. I took a cleansing breath, ridding myself of the heaviness. I took the opportunity to look around, looking for a place to run and hide, a place that might offer escape. I got to my feet and ran to the nearest room.

When I opened the door, I recognized my old room. Pink walls, princess border, and my pink comforter with Roscoe propped on the pillow. Slowly—slowly— everything started to fall into place.

The ghost in the blue dress and I had been sitting on the balcony in my old house. I didn't even recognize it.

The place where she fell to her death.

I walked back to the area where we had played dolls, thinking, trying to form a plan of escape. How could I escape from her world? But what if I was dead? I wasn't sure, but an idea formed as I turned in a small circle, taking in my surroundings.

The dream I had of her last night flashed through my mind. If she could fall to her death, could I? I turned to the second-floor banister. My little hands pulled and my little legs scrambled until I was standing on top, over-looking the empty living room. It was hard to keep my balance. The black dress shoes were slick, the banister round.

Sadness, loneliness, and confusion took over again. The ghost in the blue dress was back with more tea. I could feel her presence behind me.

"Sissy?" Her voice sounded eerie. "Sissy, come stay with me." She stomped her foot. The ghost in the blue dress either thought I was her sister or wanted me to be her sister. I wasn't sure, and it made me feel a little sorry for her.

But I wasn't the ghost's sister, and I wouldn't be happy living her in her world, wherever this was. I wanted to go home, to be with my mom, to be with my new friends, and Zane.

I looked back over my shoulder, and teetered for a moment on the banister, my shoes slick against the polished round surface. Then—I let go.

"Sissy!"

༺༻

"Jenna!"

The blackness faded for a moment. Was someone there? But the blackness returned. I felt something on my face, wet and cold. I raised my hand to touch it, but I was too weak. I lowered my hand to rest on my stomach.

"Jenna!"

I tried to open my eyes but couldn't.

The same voice again. "Jenna!"

Who could that be? Did you hear voices when you were dead?

The heaviness slowly lifted, and my eyelids fluttered open, lifting the fog that had imprisoned me. A person bent over me. Mom.

"She's awake," she said into her phone.

"What—" I managed to get out. I struggled to sit. "What happened?"

"Just stay still, honey," she said. "The ambulance is on its way. Don't move."

Ambulance? I lay back down. The back of my head throbbed, causing a memory to replay in my mind. I needed to find the dress. Mom's room. Closet. A book hitting me in the back of the head, flying objects, locked door. Trapped. Completely trapped. And finally the quilt wrapping around me, squeezing me.

I jerked. My eyes went wide. I struggled to sit only to feel the quilt wrapped tight around me. I kicked at it. "Let me out!"

Mom's hands shot out to hold me still. "Calm down, honey. You've got to calm down."

After I had freed myself from the quilt, I stood, on guard, searching the room for the ghost. Another memory from earlier.

I hadn't found the dress.

CHAPTER 24

"You again?" said the same emergency room doctor, Dr. Robbins.

I tried to nod, but the paramedic had put a thing around my neck, so I couldn't move. "Hi," I managed to say, even though it sounded a bit strangled.

He walked up to the side of my bed and frowned. "What happened this time?"

I didn't know what to say. Mom sat in a chair next to me, so it wasn't like I could tell the truth. Instead of going home, I'd be sent for a psychiatric evaluation.

The doctor must've seen my attention go to her because the next question surprised me. "Mrs. Moores, could you leave us for a moment? I would like to speak with Jenna alone."

Alone. There was that word again. I swallowed and

searched the ceiling of the hospital room. No answers
there. The blood pressure machine inflated, counting
down the seconds to the interrogation. I could only imagine what my pulse was doing.

Finally, Mom stood. She hesitated for a moment,
contemplating the effects of leaving me, but the doctor
ordered her out.

The sound of the blood pressure machine filled the
silence. Dr. Robbins paced from one side of my bed to
the other, looking at my chart.

"Let's see," he said and lowered his voice a little,
giving me a sense of confidentiality. "First we had a knife
injury that I stitched up. Then a fish hook in your hand. I
can understand those being accidents. But this? I'm not
sure what we have."

I cleared my throat. I really wanted a drink of water
and the thing around my neck seemed to be getting tighter.

"Can you tell me what happened now that your
Mom's out of the room?" he asked.

And there it was, the question that I didn't want to
answer.

I'd begged Mom to tell the paramedics that I was
okay and to leave, but she didn't. She didn't know what
happened, and neither did I. So how was I supposed to
explain this to Dr. Robbins?

"Okay," he said. "Let's try something else. Who was
home when you cut your hand?"

I couldn't hold him off for long, so I decided to answer. "Mom."

"Now, who was home when you got the fish hook in your hand?"

I went back to that night and remembered that I lied and said I had been home. "Mom."

He paused for a moment. "Now, who was home today?"

"No one."

"No one?"

I tried to nod but couldn't, so I said, "Yes. No one."

"So your Mom left you at home by yourself today?"

"Yes."

"Why?"

I felt like I was on trial. My pulse raced and the thing around my neck tightened. "Because I was sick."

"You don't have a temperature and all your vitals are fine."

"I just didn't feel good."

"So your Mom let you stay home because you just didn't feel well?" He stood beside my bed, rubbing his chin. He looked deep in thought. "So what happened when she left?"

A chill raced over me followed by a wave of heat. I began to sweat beneath the thin white sheet. "I don't remember."

"Come on, Jenna, level with me here. Help me out. I am required by law to report any suspicious findings—"

"Suspicious findings?"

"Yes. If I suspect that you're being neglected or abused—"

"Mom loves me," I said, my voice slow and soft. "She'd never do anything to hurt me."

"Then tell me what happened today," he said, leaning over me.

His eyes bore into me, pressing me to tell the truth. Something inside of me just wanted to blurt it out, unload the burden that I've been carrying all these months.

The wall was about to come down when I felt the presence of the ghost. The air changed, heavy and oppressive. Even though I couldn't raise my head, I could still see a blue glow off to my right, behind Dr. Robbins.

He straightened, squinted his eyes, quickly glanced behind him. He looked for a moment before turning back to me. "That's the strangest thing." He glanced behind him again. "I could have sworn someone was behind me, but I didn't hear the door open."

The last time I'd seen that confused look was when I'd told Mrs. V about the ghost. The pink color of his face began to pale. When I met his gaze, I could tell he knew something wasn't right. And hopefully he knew it didn't have anything to do with Mom.

එ�ථ�ථ

Later that night, the doctor discharged me from the

emergency room. I lay on my bed in the dark, clutching Roscoe to my chest. What was I going to do? The ghost tried to kill me and keep me in her world, a world somewhere distant and lonely. I needed to kill her before she killed me, but I needed help. Asking for help would endanger that person, though. Who would be strong enough? Or knowledgeable enough? A name popped into my head.

Kat.

Tomorrow, Friday, I would go to school like a normal teenager and try to talk with her. Maybe she would have some sympathy for my situation and hopefully help. I couldn't get my hopes up, though. She refused to speak with me before. What made me think she'd speak with me now? But the ghost tried to kill me. That was reason enough, wasn't it?

But what if the ghost came back tonight to finish me?

My bedroom door creaked open as the idea crossed my mind. I stiffened.

"Jenna," Mom said in a soft voice. "Are you awake?"

"Yes."

Mom had just checked on me five minutes ago. "I'm sorry, honey," she said. She came into my room and sat at the foot of my bed. "I just can't leave you alone. I'm worried."

"I'm fine, Mom. Really."

She reached out and gave my foot a squeeze. "I want you sleep with me in my bed tonight."

I wanted to. I was scared. Even though I was a teenager, I didn't want to sleep alone in my own room. But after what happened today, I couldn't take a chance. I couldn't endanger Mom.

"That's okay. My bed's a lot softer than yours."

"Then I'll sleep on the floor in here with you."

"You can't." It popped out before I could stop myself.

"Why not?"

What could I say that she would believe? I paused for a moment before answering. "Because you snore, and you'll keep me awake." My foot jerked. The truth was I'd never heard her snore at all, but that was the only thing I could think of.

She let out a snort and lightly patted my leg. "I do not!"

"Yep," I said and nodded, the action bringing back the headache I'd had earlier.

She sighed, pausing for a moment. "I need to know what really happened today."

My heart rate took off, and my face flushed. There it was. The question I did not want to answer. Since I'd left the hospital, I'd been trying to come up with another explanation to explain the mess in her bedroom.

And the explanation was something so farfetched, it just might explain some other things. Not everything, but enough to buy me some time to find the dress and destroy it.

"You'll never believe me," I said, my voice flat.

"Try me, honey. I really need some answers here."

I let out an exaggerated sigh, like I was getting ready to confess a deep secret. "I don't want to tell you. You'll laugh at me."

"Tell me."

I paused again, letting the silence stretch for emphasis. "I was sleep walking," I said softly. No response. "See," I said, my tone sharp with an accusing edge to it. "I knew you wouldn't believe me." She took in a breath as if she were going to say something but didn't. "Think about it," I said. "That would explain why you found me tangled up in my curtains, right? And what about when Grandma and Grandpa were here, and I took a nap. Then I ended up on the floor." I let out a small laugh. "That was embarrassing."

She straightened. "Are you serious?"

The room was dark with only a small amount of light shining through the crack in the door. I could see her profile, her wrinkled forehead like she was thinking. She was always the one to worry and be protective. Now it was my turn. If I couldn't get her to believe me, if I couldn't get her to stay away, I may not be able to protect her through the night.

"I'm totally serious, Mom. I've known about it for a while, since at the old house, but I wasn't sure how to bring it up. But it's getting worse, so maybe you should take me to the doctor. Make an appointment with a sleep specialist or something." I yawned, long and drawn out. "I'm exhausted. Just go to bed and check on me later. No big deal."

She sat for a moment longer. All of my effort went into that last explanation. It was all I had.

Finally, she stood and leaned forward, kissing me on the forehead. "I believe you, sweetheart. I'll call tomorrow and get you in before the weekend. I don't think I could handle another emergency room visit." My shoulders relaxed and my heart rate began to ease back to normal. She believed me. "Make sure to turn off your alarm. No use waking up early since you're staying home again." Then she left, closing the door to the hallway light.

Since tomorrow was Friday, I had no choice but to go to school and talk with Kat. If I didn't talk to her before the weekend and find out what I had to do, I might not be here Monday. I might be a ghost.

I reached over and checked my alarm. It was set. Then I reached under my pillow and put my velvet sleeping mask on. Maybe if I went to sleep, maybe if I didn't do anything like search for the dress or anything that the ghost might not like, she'd leave me alone.

CHAPTER 25

And the ghost did leave me alone. The next morning my alarm went off, and I sat on the edge of the bed. The back of my head throbbed and my body felt like I'd been run over by a supernatural freight train. Every muscle and every nerve wanted me to take another pain pill and lie back down, pulling the blankets over my eyes to block out the bright sun. But I knew I couldn't. I needed to get to school.

With my mask still on, I listened. No sounds came from the hallway or anywhere else in the house. Mom must still have been asleep.

I hurried to the bathroom and hopped in the shower, taking care not to drop anything and cause extra noise. When I shampooed my hair, my fingers ran over the lump on the back of my head. I winced. The knot was extremely sore and alarmingly large. No wonder the doctor was concerned. Once I was finished and dried off, I made my way to my room to get dressed.

After staring at my clock until it was time for the bus, I snuck out of my room and into the kitchen to leave a note. I pulled a pen from the drawer, but before I even made my first letter, I heard a voice.

"Just where do you think you're going?"

My stomach flipped and my arms tingled from being startled. Mom entered the kitchen from the dark hallway. Her hair was still up in a ponytail and her mascara was smudged at the corners of her eyes. Was it from sleeping or had she been crying? I hoped it was from sleeping.

I put the pen down since there was no need to leave a note now. "I'm going to school."

"No you're not."

"I have to."

"No you don't."

"I have my first test in algebra, and I can't miss it. I was going to leave you a note. See?" I held up the paper.

"You're going to see a specialist today." She walked over to me and took my book bag. "Now just relax and watch TV or something. I'll make us some breakfast." I glanced at the clock. The bus would be here any minute. "I called the emergency room last night and talked with that doctor you saw. I told him." She glanced at me over her shoulder and then cracked an egg into the skillet. "I told him what you told me last night about sleep walking, and he has a friend who is a sleep specialist. He said he'd get you in today. He seemed very eager to help. I think he was worried about you."

I listened for the bus. "Can you pick me up from school then? After my test?"

"Honey, just stay home."

"My test is first period. Just pick me up afterwards. Please."

"This must be some test."

"It is, Mom. If I don't pass this, it'll affect my grade for the rest of the semester." The bus approached. The winding down of the engine and the squeak of the brakes spurred me into action. "I'll be waiting outside the main doors."

I shuffled over to the stove and gave her a quick kiss on the cheek. Before she could say anything further, I grabbed my bag and headed for the door.

I had to talk with Kat and try to convince her to help me. The uneventful night actually scared me. What was the ghost in the blue dress up to? Was she saving up her energy for the final showdown?

✂✎✂

Sam skipped over to me, her spiked blonde hair un-moving. "Guess what!"

"What?" I had to answer even though I didn't want to. I wanted to get to algebra class.

"No. Seriously. Guess."

"Sam, I don't have time for this," I said, regretting the words as soon as they popped out.

She narrowed her eyes. "Well, just thought you would like to know that Zane was coming back today." She spun on her heel and walked away.

I should have felt relief. The fact that Zane was coming back to school was great news, but the fact that the ghost was still around wasn't. And if I didn't destroy her soon, who knew if she might hurt him again? I couldn't stand it.

When I walked into class, Kat sat in her usual seat, book open, studying.

"Kat," I said and sat beside her. I scooted my desk a little closer. She glanced up for just a moment before looking at her book again. "I need your help."

"I've already helped you as much as I can. Now leave me alone." Her words were low, coming through gritted teeth.

"But I tried to find the link, the dress, and she attacked me. I spent all evening in the emergency room." My voice rose a notch, and my words tumbled out. "I don't know what else to do. She's getting stronger, and I'm afraid. Please help me."

Kat looked up from her book for a moment. Had I convinced her? But then she closed it and stood and walked to the door. "Kat!" I followed her into the hall as everyone else came in.

The halls were mostly empty. The warning bell rang.

"Kat, wait," I said. The only person that could even come close to helping me was walking away.

She stopped suddenly before we reached the cafeteria. The sound of voices and feet shuffling from students still lingered. She turned, her long dark hair swinging. "Leave me alone!" Her finger shook as she pointed it at me, accusing me.

"Just tell me what to do."

"I already have."

"But I don't know where the link is, and when I searched for it, she attacked me." My voice cracked, and I felt my eyes water. "I thought it was over. That she'd won. Then I finally woke up. My mom is scared that something's wrong with me, and I came to school today so I could talk with you." I took in a deep breath, willing the tears back. "You're the only person who can help me right now," I said, hoping she could hear me, because I could barely hear myself.

Kat threw her bag down. "You have no idea what you're messing with do you? That ghost is powerful, and I don't want anything to do with it or with you!"

I lowered my head and looked at the floor. All of the hope that I had left, all of the fight I had left was gone— gone with Kat's refusal to help me.

Maybe I should just give up, let the ghost kill me and live in her world.

That was what she wanted.

I turned around, ready to go back to algebra for my bag, so that I could go wait for Mom outside.

"Wait," Kat said suddenly.

I stopped.

"You have to burn the link she has to this world. You think it's the dress?"

I turned to face her. "I know it's the dress now. I had a dream that she and her sister both died in blue dresses, but she won't let me find it."

"Does anyone know where it's at?"

My hope started to come back. "Mom."

"Then you need to ask her."

"But I can't. The ghost will hurt her."

"It's the only way to stop her."

Kat stared at me for a moment before I noticed the change in the air. She felt it too, because her eyes widened in fear. Then she jerked backward, her arms flying forward like she had been pushed in the chest.

"Kat!" I ran to her and grabbed her arms to steady her. What was happening?

"Help," she whispered.

Her normally rich voice sounded raspy and her eyes seemed to lose focus. One second they were pleading with me and the next they were staring at nothing. She started to sway. She swayed so far to one side that she just about fell.

"Someone help!" My voice echoed through the hall and into the cafeteria. Voices responded. Feet pounded the floor. "Kat!" I said again, hoping her eyes would focus on me. But then her deep brown eyes faded in color until they were white.

Entirely white.

My head swam. I felt faint. I watched Kat's eyelids close, and her body went limp. Another student was suddenly by my side, carefully lowering her to the floor.

Another voice. "Call 911."

I stepped back.

"What happened?" they asked.

I shook my head. I didn't know what happened. A flash of Mrs. V, now lying in the nursing home, waiting to recover. It was a stroke the doctors said. My fault. And now Kat. *What have I done?*

I felt faint. Arms grabbed me, steadying me. Voices again.

"Are you all right?"

The arms sat me on the floor. I lowered my head. *Think*, I told myself. *What do I do? What do I do now? The only thing I can do.*

Burn the dress.

❧❧❧

I burst through the main doors of the high school, leaving Kat behind. *I have to save her.* And Mrs. V. And Zane. And me. Still unsteady, I looked up. Not sure what I was looking for, maybe an answer or some type of clue.

Instead, I saw white clouds racing across the sky, like they were running from something. Thunder. Distant and angry. And I knew what they were running from.

A car horn honked, tearing my attention away from the sky. I glanced at the parking lot. Mom! She was early. I rushed down the stairs.

"Where's your bag, honey?" she asked when I climbed in.

"We need to talk."

She raised her eyebrows. "I'm listening."

An image of Kat's white eyes flashed through my mind, and I paused. If I told Mom, then the ghost would hurt her. What if the ghost hurt her before she told me what I needed to know?

Mom cleared her throat. "What is it, Jenna? You know you can tell me."

"Can we go home first?"

"We don't have time. Your appointment's in an hour."

"We really have to go home."

"We really—"

"I peed my pants."

Silence.

I turned toward her. The crow's feet around her eyes were more pronounced than normal and her bottom lip sucked in, gnawing away on the inside. The rich brown that she had colored her hair earlier had faded into a dull tone, making her look years older.

Or was it the stress that I'd put on her that made her look older? Either way she looked like she was going to have a breakdown of her own if she didn't learn the truth soon.

"Mom, I promise to tell you everything, and I mean everything, if you drive me home now. Fast."

She held my stare for a moment. In that moment, I wondered if I'd lost her already, not to the ghost but to the awful summer that she endured. Between the death of her husband and dealing with an awful teenage daughter, the truth might hurt her more than save her. But when she reached down and put the TrailBlazer in drive, turning out of the parking lot toward home, I knew I no longer had a choice.

CHAPTER 26

When we finally pulled into the driveway, the thunder clouds had surrounded us, black and angry. I unlatched my seatbelt and turned to face Mom. It was time to tell her the truth.

"I promised to tell you everything," I said, pausing for a moment before continuing. The blood pounded through my veins. "I swear this is the honest truth, and I need you to help me and answer my questions even if you don't believe me. Promise?"

Her face was unreadable in the dim light, but her voice soft. "Promise."

"There's been a ghost haunting me since Dad died." I waited for it to sink in before I continued. "I'd seen her when I was a kid, but then she disappeared." I waved my hand through the air. "Now she's back and she's extreme-ly dangerous. She hurt Mrs. V, Zane, and now my friend Kat from school. And she's going to hurt you, too, now that I've told you about her."

Mom remained silent.

"I'm not crazy, Mom. I'm telling you the truth. She wears that little blue dress that you had my picture taken in when I was little."

She gasped.

I straightened. "What? What do you know?"

"It can't be," she said and brought a trembling hand up to brush the bangs from her eyes.

I still couldn't read her expression. "Tell me what you know, Mom. Tell me where the dress is, so I can burn it. It's the only way to destroy the ghost."

Then I felt the change.

Even though I knew it was coming, the sudden change in the air sent chills racing across my body just like the clouds racing across the sky. Heaviness wrapped around us.

"Is that what you were looking for last night?"

"Yes, but I couldn't find it, and then she attacked me." I grabbed her arm. "I have to destroy that dress, Mom. Kat's in danger *right now* and the ghost, she's get-ting stronger. She almost killed me last night."

The air started to churn, slowly at first, but then building momentum like a spinning vortex. Receipts, loose dirt, and a lone paper clip spun through the air, around and around and around. The loose dirt peppered us. My hair blew across my face.

Mom grabbed my hand. "It's in my closet," she said over the sound of the churning air and threw open her door. I followed. We ran into the house and down the hall, toward her bedroom, toward the little blue dress.

We crashed through her bedroom door. The hairs on my arms and neck stood. She pulled two large boxes from the closet. The hair on my head rose as if I had rubbed a balloon on it.

"Hurry, Mom!"

Finally, she pulled out a third box, one that the little ghost didn't let me get to last night.

But just when Mom started to open it, she coughed and her hands shot to her neck.

"Mom!" I fell to her side.

She was choking! I searched for something to pull away from her neck, but there wasn't anything there. Mom's eyes widened, like they were going to burst. She tried to suck in a breath of air, but an awful groaning noise came out instead.

I knelt over her, trying to fight something that was more powerful than I. Something I couldn't see. Something I couldn't touch. How was I supposed to help her?

Burn the dress.

That was the only way I could win. Frantically, I turned to the box and started digging, pulling out things and throwing them off to the side. Item after item after item pulled from the box. Just as I started to doubt the dress was even there, I found it.

A surge of relief shot through my body. The blue dress. I wanted to crush it to my chest and cry. Now that I had the dress, everything was going to be okay. Mom was going to be okay—as soon as I burned it.

With a firm grip on the dress, I ran for the bedroom door. But just when I reached it, the door slammed shut, just like yesterday. When I pulled on the door knob, it wouldn't budge, just like yesterday. And when I turned around, everything in the room hovered inches from its surface, just like yesterday.

The items were waiting to attack me, waiting to kill me.

I stood with my back to the locked door. Mom lay on the floor with her hands around her throat, legs kicking wildly. I glanced around the dim room. The deep angry growl of thunder echoed throughout the room followed by a flash of lightning.

It lit up the room, coming through the bedroom window above the cedar chest. It flashed again, like it was trying to draw my attention to the window.

The window.

That's how I would escape! Without hesitating, I sprang across Mom's bed to the other side and picked up the lamp on her nightstand.

With one hand gripping the dress and the other gripping the lamp, I jumped on top of the cedar chest and started to swing the lamp to break the window. But before the lamp hit the glass, an object struck me in the ribs. My body arched to the side, and I dropped the lamp. Pain. Another object pelted the back of my leg. I lost my balance.

I fell to my knees. Item after item hit my body. I rolled onto my side and covered my head. I had a strange feeling, like something big was coming. Something that would hurt. The hairs on my neck tingled, and I braced myself.

Mom's jewelry box whizzed by my head. It was so close, I could feel the movement of the air. It hit the window, shattering a hole in the glass. Wind and rain blew through the broken window. But the break wasn't big enough for me to get through. I spun around and kicked out with my feet. One foot after the other. I shattered the entire window pane.

Quickly, I got to my knees. The wind picked up speed, whipping through the room. I could hear Mom cough. Glass clinked and tinkled under my shifting weight. I had to dive through the window. Pieces of glass whirled through the air in a circular motion, like a spinning vortex. A strong gust of wind blew the curtains up and out, similar to the night my curtains tried to kill me. Before they could surround me and squeeze me to death, I dove.

I dove out the broken window.

I landed on my stomach on the rain-soaked ground.

The air in my lungs was forced out. A searing pain tore through my chest. I opened my mouth to suck in precious oxygen, but there was nothing—only rain pelting my face and body.

Normally, I would have screamed. Instead, I could only whimper. Was this it? Was this how I would die?

At first the steady rhythm of raindrops was bothersome, almost painful on my beaten limbs. But after a moment, the pain passed and the raindrops grew comforting, almost like they were lulling me to sleep.

Get up.

My lips formed the words. No sound.

Get up.

Or Mom will die.

Get up.

Or I will die.

My body felt like it had been sucked into the mud, unable to move. I forced my shoulder up off the ground. Next, I forced my hand and arm to move and push my body up and over. I turned onto my back. Now with my weight off my arm, a stinging pain shot up to my shoulder. Warm blood flowed from my forearm.

I glanced down. A jagged tear ran from my elbow, curving toward my wrist. Bright red blood stained the blue dress. The front of my shirt was dirty and torn. Now that my arm was free, the blood flowed unbridled. My eyes wanted to close. I wanted to forget. Forget this awful summer. Forget this lonely life of mine.

But I couldn't. Not when Mom was fighting for her life only feet from me. And Kat was in trouble back at school.

And what about Mrs. V?

Get up.

Determined, I rolled onto my stomach and pulled my legs up and underneath me. With my good arm, I pushed myself to my feet, staggering in the light rain. With the dress still in my hand, I made my way toward the garage.

Too weak to manage opening the main garage door, I stumbled through the front door of the living room, still open from when Mom and I barged in just moments ago. When I finally made it down the hall and to the garage, I threw open the door. I needed lighter fluid and a lighter.

Now.

I started across the garage floor. A few more steps—

But before I took those few more steps, I saw her. The ghost in the blue dress appeared in the corner of the garage near the workbench. Her blue dress almost glowed in the dim light of the garage, dim from the midday thunderstorm. Her wavy hair draped in front of her shoulders, covering some of the white lace. She looked almost innocent, except for her eyes.

I tore myself from her stare and searched the counter for the lighter fluid and lighter. I gasped. There they were, sitting by the grill where Mom had left them. My heart thumped hard against my chest. I was so close. But so was she.

I needed to get my hands on those things or Mom would die. This spurred me into action, and I lunged, grabbing the lighter fluid, fumbling for a moment before getting a good grip. I threw the dress down and drenched it as quickly as possible.

The bottle flew from my hands, sending a stream of lighter fluid all over my arm. Quickly, I turned and grabbed the lighter. But before I could ignite it, it flew from my hands and skidded across the cement garage floor along with my heart. No, no, no.

No!

I ran toward the lighter and dove. The impact against the cement floor pushed the air from my body. I couldn't breathe, but I really didn't care. I had the lighter in my hand.

I struggled to my feet and turned toward the dress, finger ready to click the lighter to life. But just as I took that first step, I felt two small hands against my chest as if the ghost were pushing me away.

Away from the dress.

"Sissy!"

Her small voice, only sounding in my head, held a note of surprise. My heart twisted.

But I pushed forward, toward the dress. "I am not your sister!"

"*Sissy*!" The hands pushed harder as if she could convince me to stop and listen.

"I am not your sister!" I yelled again and threw my

arms out like I could fight her. The force pushing against me didn't budge. I leaned forward again, straining, pushing. *I must get to the dress. I must burn the dress. I must destroy the dress.*

But it was like pushing against a brick wall. My feet slipped out of my sandals. This wasn't working. I had to do something else. But what?

I remembered last year when I tried out for the basketball team, a maneuver to get around the opponent and get to the basket. Without really thinking it through, because I didn't really have time, I lowered my right shoulder and spun. I could feel the edge of the brick wall rolling behind me.

With the wall to my back, I flung my body, arms outstretched toward the dress. Before I landed, I clicked the lighter to life. Just as I hit the floor, the small yellow flame made contact with the edge of the white lace.

The fire spread, following the zigzag pattern of lighter fluid. At first the pattern burned yellow, superficial. But it only took a moment until it burned true blue.

Flames danced, looking similar to one another in one second but then different in another. I rolled to the side, away from the fire. I watched the flames destroy the dress for just a second.

It was over now. Now I needed to see Mom. Make sure she was okay.

But I couldn't get up. Then, suddenly, I couldn't breathe. At first I thought the smoke from burning the dress caused it, but it only took a second before I realized it was the ghost.

Fear shot through my chest. I tried to suck in air, but it was as if invisible hands were wrapped around my neck. I kicked my feet and thrashed my arms.

Nothing.

I fought and fought and fought.

But she wouldn't let go. She was going to kill me yet.

Slowly, as if I were entering a tunnel, darkness crowded the edges of my vision, crowding the sight of the burning dress until it was gone.

Until everything was gone.

I wasn't sure how long I lay on the garage floor. Time seemed to stop, the darkness comforting. But it wasn't the darkness that was comforting. It was the sensation of being hugged. Arms wrapped around me, giving me a sense of peace, of closure. I knew that hug. I'd missed that hug. I'd believed I would never feel that hug again.

Dad.

I wanted to talk to him, ask him things about death and the afterlife. What was it like? Did it hurt? Was he happy? What was Heaven like? But the words didn't come.

I felt only the comfort of his hug. And then, too soon, it was gone.

A faint noise broke through the darkness, something

echoing within the garage walls. It sounded like a child laughing. It was the ghost.

"Sissy!" her tiny thin voice said.

My gut twisted for a moment, thinking she was calling to me. But then I heard another child laughing. Two small children laughed and giggled together. The darkness that had swallowed my vision started to fade, starting from the center, spreading outward until I could see everything again. The garage. The burning dress.

And I could breathe again. Air rushed into my lungs, expanding them until it felt like they were going to burst.

The air whooshed in and out of them freely. I still couldn't move. My body hurt. My soul hurt. I needed to see Mom. Make sure she was okay.

A small part of me felt sorry for the ghost in the blue dress, the way she lost her sister, the way she died, the way she was lost between here and there—wherever that might be.

The fire was slowly dying, fading into nothing, just like the voices of the happy little sisters.

CHAPTER 27

The noon sun was shining bright now that the storm had passed. I turned my head and glanced out of the large open garage door. My chest and ribs hurt. Each blade of grass glistened from the rain, the gravel road wet. Fresh air blew across my face, blowing the ashes from the dress gently in different directions. Just a hint of rain remained.

A hand brushed the hair from my face. "Oh, honey. Am I going to have to take you to the emergency room again?" Mom asked.

She survived, and so did I! I destroyed the ghost in the blue dress. My eyes moistened, and I smiled.

"Just lie still. The ambulance is on its way," she said and patted my shoulder. I reached for her hand.

Once we arrived at the hospital, they tried to take us

to separate rooms, but I wouldn't let go of her. "Don't leave me," I said to her.

"Never."

After they wheeled in another bed, we waited together for the doctor. "What are we going to say?" I finally asked.

"I'm not sure. We'll think of something, I guess."

I reached up and rubbed my temple. I had so many questions about the ghost now that she was reunited with her sister. And the letter. I knew now wasn't the time, but I had to ask. "Mom?"

"What, honey?"

"I found the letter Dad wrote to me."

She sucked in a quick breath of air. "Oh my gosh. I forgot about the letter." She tightened her grip. "He knew, didn't he?"

"I believe so. He was trying to warn me."

"I'm so sorry, Jenna. I thought it would upset you. It didn't sound like your father at all."

"I understand, Mom. You didn't know, but one thing I still don't understand is the dress."

"Actually," she said, "it must've been her dress. It was hanging in the closet in your room when we moved in. It was just there, all by itself..." She trailed off, remembering. "Just so beautiful. When I opened the closet door, the sun hit it at just the right angle, and it almost glowed, so breathtaking. And it happened to be just your size." She paused for a moment. "The following week, I took you to get your picture taken in it."

I remembered the vision of the twin sister dying in my room. When the ghost tried to kill me, I was wearing a matching blue dress. And the ghost always called me Sissy. I gasped. "It was her sister's dress."

∽∂∽

Later that afternoon Dr. Robbins released us from the hospital after a few X-rays. He knew something beyond his belief system caused the damage, because he didn't ask very many questions. He did stitch the cut in my arm, though, and I had a broken rib. I think we both hoped we didn't see each other for a long time.

While there, I checked on another patient.

Kat.

"Hey," I said when I walked into her room.

She glanced at my bandaged arm. "So?"

"The ghost is gone," I said and sat in one of the chairs. Mom sat in the other. "Mom, this is Kat. She told me how to get rid of the ghost." I turned to Kat. "This is my mom, Debra."

They exchanged greetings and then Mom said, "I'm so sorry, Kat, that you got hurt in all this mess."

"I'm fine, really. Are you guys okay?"

Mom and I looked at each other. "We're together," Mom said, "and that's all that matters."

Kat nodded. "I agree."

Then her parents walked in. We said hello but that we needed to go.

"See you next week," I said.

"Better have your algebra done," Kat said and gave me an *everything-is-fine-now* smile.

Now that I knew Kat was going to be okay, we left. I guessed she told the doctor that she didn't eat breakfast and felt sick before she passed out. He decided to check her sugar levels along with some other tests.

⁊⁊⁊

Early Saturday morning, I got up and showered, taking care of the new stitches. Dr. Robbins had removed the old ones in my hand from the knife cut while I was there yesterday. I had to go back in two weeks to have these removed. Maybe I'd tell him what happened, what *really* happened, if he wanted to hear it.

I dressed slowly, taking my time with my sore chest and ribs. My body ached, but I was determined. After I tried to pull my hair up into a ponytail, a knock sounded on my door. It was Mom, dressed and ready. She came in and helped me fix my hair. We hadn't even discussed what we were going to do today, but here we were, ready to leave.

Before I left my room, I went to my top dresser and opened it. I found Mrs. V's Precious Moments in the back of the drawer, wrapped tight to keep it safe. I held it in my hands for the five-hour drive to the nursing home in Cleveland, Ohio.

I couldn't wait to see Mrs. V as we walked down the hall to her room, 12B. She had crossed my mind so many times. So many times, I couldn't forgive myself for getting her into this mess. But now it was over. I just hoped she was the same person she used to be.

A pang hit me in the stomach. I must've flinched, because Mom reached over and put her arm around me. "Everything will be just fine, honey. You'll see." The sound of a little dog barking floated down the hall. Pepe! He must've heard Mom's voice.

When we walked into Mrs. V's room, she looked up. Her eyes were bright. Her cheeks were bright. And her smile was bright and warm. It was so warm, it dissolved the discomfort that had formed in my stomach.

I returned her smile with one of my own and made my way to the side of her bed. I unwrapped her figurine and placed it on her nightstand.

"Oh, dear," Mrs. V said in a soft whisper and held out her arms for a hug.

Pepe jumped onto the bed and licked Mrs. V's cheek. I leaned down and wrapped my arms around her. We held each other for a long time. I could feel that she'd lost weight and had become more fragile than she looked. A sick feeling made my stomach roll. How many years had I taken from her? How many more years would she have lived if I hadn't asked her for help?

I had to say it. "I'm so sorry," I whispered against her soft white hair.

"Nonsense!" she said.

I pulled away, looking at her like I didn't understand. "But it's all my fault."

"Nonsense again. This is not your fault, my dear. This is beyond both of us." Then she nodded in a firm way. "Now. I've got to know. What happened?"

I looked at Mom. "Well, the short story is that I destroyed the ghost."

Mrs. V grabbed my hand and squeezed. "How did you do it? That ghost had been there for a long time from what I found out from Gladys. I'd always thought there was something strange about that place."

"What do you mean?"

"After I came around yesterday, I called Gladys. If you ever need to know anything, call her." Mrs. V giggled a little before she continued. "She told me about two little girls who lived there, twins. It was a long time ago, maybe fifty or sixty years. Anyway, one of the little girls got sick, pneumonia I think, and she died. Then, wrought with despair, the other little girl jumped from the balcony and committed suicide."

"It wasn't suicide. And it wasn't pneumonia." I patted Mrs. V's hand, glad to see her with so much energy. "She didn't mean to fall. She was just trying to reach out to her sister who she had accidentally poisoned. To hold her hand again."

Her forehead wrinkled as she brought up her eyebrows in surprise. "And how do you know that?"

"She showed me in kind of a dream, I guess. Her sister was thirsty, and she got her something to drink. I'm not sure what it was, but it couldn't have been water. She didn't show me that part, but I read something about two girls and an accidental poisoning. I read it at the library in an old newspaper."

We sat for a moment in silence. I was glad to be there, to be talking with Mrs. V. She took a deep breath and her expression turned serious. "I have an important question for you, dear."

After all that had happened, I had no idea what she wanted to ask. "Okay."

"Will you take care of Pepe for me if he needs it?" she asked. I gasped. She patted my hand. "Now, now, calm down. I'm not planning on leaving anytime soon. I know he loves the grandkids and all, but I think he loves you more."

I looked down at Pepe, curled up between Mrs. V and me, his little ears moving at the sound of our voices.

I swallowed the sadness forming in my throat. "I promise."

With her age, and with us living five hours away, it was possible that I might not ever see her again. Tears filled my eyes. Mrs. V reached up and smoothed my hair for a moment and then patted my arm.

I took in a shaky breath. "I have something else to tell you."

"And what's that?"

"You know how I said I believed in ghosts?" She nodded. "I believe in Heaven, too."

Her hand tightened and her eyes widened just a little before they returned to normal. Mrs. V took in a slow breath. "What happened?"

"Dad hugged me." I glanced at Mom sitting in a chair by the window. I hadn't told her about this yet. She flinched and her eyes started to shine, reflecting the soft afternoon sunlight. "The ghost almost won. She choked me until I blacked out. It was weird. Really weird. It was like I was suspended in the dark. Then I felt warm, comforting arms wrap around me. His arms. I think he was protecting me. Just like he said he would."

Mom let out a choking sob. Mrs. V's face scrunched and she took in a couple of shaky breaths. Tears slid from her eyes. "Oh, dear."

She pulled me to her chest and squeezed. A sharp pain shot through my ribs, but I didn't pull away. I'd never pull away from Mrs. V.

Once we were done hugging, I went to Mom and knelt in front of her. "It's okay, Mom. Really."

She wrapped her arms around me and pulled me close. "I can't stand the thought of losing you. I just can't." She sucked in a quivering breath. "I don't think I could take it."

"It's over now, Mom," I said. "I'm okay."

When I pulled away from Mom, Pepe was waiting by my feet. His big round eyes were sad and worried. I picked him up and held him close. He nuzzled into the crook of my neck, like he was hugging me back, his fur soft.

I couldn't believe how much I'd missed him. I couldn't believe how much I'd missed Mrs. V. I couldn't believe how much had happened this summer.

And I couldn't believe how my life was never going to be the same.

CHAPTER 28

Sunday afternoon, after we had finished lunch, the doorbell rang. Grandma and Grandpa had come to visit. I wasn't sure how Grandma felt toward me since her last visit, but she gave me a huge hug and a kiss and seemed pretty excited about something. Then Grandpa took my hand and led me out through the kitchen to the barn.

"I know how hard it is to be a teenager," he said as he started to walk along the fence, inspecting it. "And so I went ahead and got something for you."

It took me a second to finally notice what he was looking at. He was looking at a mended fence. I stopped, taking it in before finally meeting his eyes. I could barely see them because his smile took up his entire face.

I squealed like a little girl and gave him a hug.

"Thanks, Grandpa! It won't be too long now, and I'll have my horse." I tried not to, but I couldn't help bouncing up and down like a little kid, clapping and giggling.

"Oh, you're welcome, honey. You're welcome."

"But—" I said when I'd stopped bouncing up and down. "When did you manage to have it fixed? Didn't it take a long time?"

"Well, since it's only a few acres, it didn't take too long. The guys did it yesterday while you were gone," he said. Then Grandpa smiled even bigger, which I didn't think was possible, and nodded toward the road behind me. When I turned around, a small horse trailer pulled into the driveway. I sucked in my breath, making my rib hurt, and grabbed his hand. He let out a chuckle and squeezed in return, as if saying, "I understand."

A large man stepped out of the driver's side and waved in our direction. I couldn't believe it! I was finally getting a horse.

The trailer door opened. And when the horse stepped out, it was as if it had stepped out of my mind and into my backyard. A palomino, just like I wanted.

"Grandpa—" I started, but couldn't find the words to finish thanking him.

He squeezed my hand again.

We met the man in the middle of the yard and he handed me the lead rope. "His name is Peppermint. Just so you know, he likes peppermints," the man said and chuckled. "Take good care of him."

"I will," I said. "I can't believe it." I looked at Grandpa. "How'd you know I wanted a palomino?"

"That was your dad's input. Before he passed on, he told your mom to make sure you got one before you grew up and went to college. Said you'd been beggin' for one since you were a little tater tot."

I smoothed Peppermints forelock and ran my hand along his neck. He put his head down and started grazing. Grandpa handed me a brush. I brushed and groomed, smoothing and shining Peppermint's coat.

The man who had brought Peppermint hadn't left yet. "I noticed you don't have a saddle," he said.

I shook my head. "I'll have to find a job to get one."

"If you're willing to come out to my horse farm on the weekends and help clean stalls, I'm sure we can work out a deal."

I stopped brushing for a moment. A job? I turned to him. "That would actually work out great."

"Your grandpa's got my number. We'll work out the details later. Make sure it's okay with your mom." He tipped his hat to Grandpa and strolled off to his truck and trailer.

ᘓᕫᘓ

Later that evening, after I'd put Peppermint in his stall and made sure he had fresh hay and water, I went to sit on the deck. The wind chimes were mostly silent with a few notes here and there. The breeze had died down for the evening, ready for the night to come.

The French doors opened. I just assumed it was Mom coming out to enjoy the evening with me. But when I smelled Zane's cologne, my heart skipped a few beats.

"Hi," he said.

My stomach sank at the sight of his arm in a cast and sling but, other than that, he looked…great. He came and sat next to me. No hint of garlic today.

"Hi," I said. I couldn't look away from his smile. He took my hand, wrapping his fingers through mine. Electric currents shot through me. "Feeling better?"

He nodded. "I am now."

ⓔⓢⓔⓢ

That night, after an evening spent with Zane and my new horse, I got ready for bed. Tomorrow was another day of school. Zane wanted me to sit with him at lunch, and Kat had invited me to go shopping with her next Saturday. After our conversation at the hospital, I thought we were going to be best friends, maybe eventually becoming as close as sisters.

I thought of Dad. Would I be reunited with him one day just like the ghost in the blue dress was reunited with her sister? I hoped so. But one thing I was sure of, Dad was there, protecting me.

I pulled my blankets up under my chin and reached

for Roscoe. I pulled him close—so many years of comfort and reassurance. But I didn't need him anymore, now that that ghost was gone. So I wrapped him safely in my pink comforter and put him gently underneath the bed.

THE END

About the Author

R. A. Slone's love for telling stories goes way back. She remembers taking pieces of paper, cutting them into squares, and stapling them together to form small books. When she was a teenager, her parents bought her a Smith Corona typewriter for Christmas, and she would stay up late at night, writing about horses galloping into the sunset. Later, after she grew up and had some life experience, she tried her hand at writing again. This time she started with short stories and eventually worked her way into writing full-length novels. She lives in Indiana with her husband and cat and is currently working on a new story.